The Ghosts Of Winworth Manor

Ann Drighton

ISBN: 978-1-6847-0748-5 (sc)
ISBN: 978-1-6847-0750-8 (hc)
ISBN: 978-1-6847-0749-2 (e)

Library of Congress Control Number: 2019909259

Lulu Publishing Services rev. date: 08/23/2019

For my beloved Barry—until God brings us together again!

Contents

Dark Obsessions

Winworth Manor
Seaside New York, 1818

"Welcome, Jason, Pauline. I do hope the two of you enjoyed your honeymoon," said Michael. "And, of course, you, Pauline, are as lovely as ever." He bent down to take her hand and kissed the back of it.

As he slowly stood up straight, his lustful eyes gazed upon her. She felt uncomfortable, as though this had been a bad mistake. She knew Michael too had fallen for her. However, she loved—and had married—his younger brother, Jason Winworth.

Michael turned and smiled at Jason. "You're a lucky man, Jason. I'm happy for the both of you."

"Thank you, Michael," replied Jason.

Why is Michael being so cordial to us? Pauline wondered.

He had shown Jason nothing but contempt and jealousy since the day Jason was born. Then Pauline had chosen Jason's proposal of marriage over Michael's, which had only furthered Michael's ire.

"Well," Michael began, "I hope you two are hungry. I have an amazing dinner planned for this evening. Shall we move to the dining room?"

As they made their way through the foyer, Pauline kept looking around the massive mansion. The black-and-white marbled foyer was breathtaking, the crowning jewel being the massive crystal chandelier that hung from the ceiling as a magnificent centerpiece. Her family, the Andrews, had plenty of wealth. But it didn't come anywhere near the Winworth estate.

The Winworths were a prosperous family who had emigrated from

England to America in 1730, just eighty-eight years prior. Jason and Michael's great-great-grandfather had been an extremely successful entrepreneur and decided to expand his enterprise to the New World. The untapped agricultural potential provided new resources that helped his businesses to flourish. When he moved his immediate family from England to the colonies, most thought he was taking too much of a gamble. However, his instincts were correct, and the family's wealth grew immensely.

After a few years, the massive Winworth Manor had been completed, and it was a symbol of the family's opulence. It had survived both the Revolutionary War and the War of 1812 and was always a reminder of how powerful the Winworth family had become.

***

The three of them made their way into the dining room, and the servants started to bring out the first course. Jason felt uneasy as he noticed that Michael couldn't keep his eyes off Pauline.

She's my wife! thought Jason. *Why must he keep gazing upon her like a carnivorous beast? Pauline and I just need to get through this evening. Then we will never have anything to do with him ever again. I was hoping this dinner could bring Michael and me closer together. But it will not. He is too self-absorbed and will never put anyone else before his own needs. He will never change. He will always be his mother's son.*

The entire evening seemed to be filled with fake smiles and disingenuous conversations. Jason noticed that even the servants seemed to feel the tension in the air. Helga, the head chambermaid, looked as though she were suffocating. She and the other servants were trapped in the unbearable situation.

Michael turned his attention back to his brother and sister-in-law.

"So, Jason, Pauline, when are the two of you going to be moving in here?"

Jason watched Pauline's eyes widen as his new wife's face turned pale. This was the one question that he had feared most of the night. There was no way that he and Pauline were moving into the manor. He didn't want Michael anywhere near her.

"Actually, Michael, Pauline's father has offered us a cottage on his estate. It's smaller than here, but it has more than ample room for a newlywed couple."

"Really?" asked Michael. "This is your home as well as your birthright. I would think you would want to live here. Don't you think Pauline deserves the best?"

"Of course I do," replied Jason. "It's just that this place means more to you than it does to me, and we would like to have a place of our own."

"The entire east wing is more than enough space for the two of you," said Michael. "This is one of the largest estates in the entire world. We would probably only see one another at mealtimes, if then. Plus, it has an amazing location and the most magnificent view, being located on the shoreline. Best of all, there are plenty of servants at your beck and call. Pauline would want for nothing. Besides, I'm sure if Father were alive, he would want you to live in the home that is also your birthright."

"I just think it would be better if Pauline and I had a place of our own," Jason replied. "Besides, I'm sure you'll find a wife soon. She may not want to live with your brother's family."

Michael just casually smiled.

"Of course," he replied. "If that is what the two of you truly want, who am I to argue? Just always remember, Brother, this is also your home. You are free to live here if the two of you ever change your minds."

***

After dinner, the servants cleared the table and finished cleaning up the dining room. It was not difficult for them to eavesdrop on the entire conversation. A collective feeling of disappointment washed over them when Jason declined his brother's offer.

They hated Michael and wished that Jason were the lord of the estate instead. Even if he wasn't, just his living there might make their lives a little easier. Michael treated them like slaves instead of his staff. He demanded their obedience and service at all times throughout the day.

"Helga," said Michael, "I would like to spend alone time with my brother and sister-in-law. You and the other servants are free to leave."

Helga almost dropped the tray of dirty dishes that she was carrying into the kitchen. Did he really just tell her they were free to leave? Was he up to something? A part of Helga wanted to stay; she knew how devious

Michael could be. Even when he was a small boy, she could see he had a darkness inside of him. He was just as bad as his wicked mother.

Helga was starting to worry about what he might be planning. If he was planning something, she knew it would be bad for either Jason or Pauline. However, she knew better than to incur Michael's wrath. There was nothing she could do to stop any of Michael's nefarious plans. Still, maybe if she stayed, Michael might be less likely to try anything.

"L-Lord Winworth," Helga began, "are-are you sure you don't need me for the rest of the evening?"

Michael's face hardened, and he slammed his fist down on the table. This made the poor woman jump, as the loud bang had startled her.

"No, Helga! I gave you an order!" Michael exclaimed. "You and the rest of the servants will retire to the servants' quarters, now! If not, I shall summon the police and have you arrested for trespassing! Is that understood?"

"Y-yes, Lord Winworth!" Helga knew that Michael did not make threats; he kept promises. Fearing him, she and the rest of the servants made their way to the front door and outside to the servants' quarters. As they were leaving, one of the other servants turned toward Helga.

"Do you think Lord Jason and Lady Pauline will be all right?" the servant girl whispered.

Helga whispered back to her, "I don't know. I'm just going to count my blessings. Be grateful that our quarters are only located in cottages outside the manor. I have a feeling something horrible is going to happen in that house tonight."

***

Jason shook his head as he watched all the servants hurry out the door.

"You were a little rude to her, Michael, don't you think?"

Michael looked at Jason with a malevolent smirk upon his face.

"A good servant needs to know her place."

"This isn't the South, Michael," said Jason. "And they aren't slaves."

Michael began to chuckle.

"Oh, my dear brother," Michael replied, "you always were an idealistic one. Now, this is a dinner that I put together to honor your's and Pauline's two-week anniversary. We should not be fighting. We should be celebrating. So, shall the three of us retire to the study?"

"Actually, Michael," Jason began, "it's getting late, and Pauline and I need to be on our way."

"Oh?" Michael inquired. "But I brought up the finest bottle of champagne from the cellar. It's chilling as we speak. You know how expensive ice can be. Please. I want to toast your nuptials."

"All right," said Jason, "but we can only stay for a little while longer."

"Of course," said Michael. "Pauline, may I?" He offered her his arm, and she reluctantly took it.

***

Pauline wanted to leave. The entire evening was causing her to feel some sort of nausea. It was as if the queasy feeling was a bad omen. She didn't trust Michael. He had been obsessed with her for the past two years. She knew he was angry at Jason and believed that he had stolen her from him. Michael had never accepted the fact that she didn't love him.

As they made their way into the study, Jason took her hand and led her to the sofa. They sat and watched Michael pour three glasses of champagne.

"I don't want to be here," Pauline whispered to Jason. "I don't trust him. He's never been nice to you. What's with this change of heart?"

"I understand how you feel," replied Jason in a low whisper, "but he is still my brother. I wanted to come here this evening, because I thought he was willing to make an effort. I wanted to give him a chance. But I was wrong. Don't worry, we'll never have to see him again after tonight."

He then gave her a quick wink. She smiled at him because she knew it was his way of signaling to her that everything was going to be all right.

Michael brought their glasses, and they both graciously thanked him.

"A toast! To the perfect blue-eyed, blond-haired couple!" Michael said, raising his glass. "May you both receive that happiness that you each so rightly deserve."

Jason and Pauline thought it was an odd toast, but they clinked glasses with him and drank the champagne.

"It's good, isn't it?" said Michael as he looked at Pauline. "It was one of our best bottles, but then Pauline always did deserve the best."

She quickly began to feel uncomfortable as a wickedly amorous smile slowly crept up on his face.

Jason's eyes widened, and he clenched his teeth as Michael kept staring at Pauline like his soon to be devoured prey. It was obvious that Jason was starting to feel anger toward his brother. It was time to leave.

"You know, Michael, this has been a nice evening," said Jason, "but Pauline and I really need to get going."

They got up off the couch and headed for the door.

Michael's ice-blue eyes darkened. Before Jason and Pauline even had a chance, Michael reached the door first. The door slammed shut, and Michael locked it with the key.

"You two aren't going anywhere," said Michael. He stood there, watching them. He was like a hungry cat who had cornered a pair of hapless mice. As tears came to Pauline's eyes, she looked at Michael, feeling nothing but fear and horror. She began to tremble, as she could see malevolence in his now darkened eyes.

"What the hell are you doing, Michael?" asked Jason.

"Taking back what's rightfully mine," Michael responded with determination in his voice. "The woman you stole from me."

"I was never yours!" cried Pauline. "You're mistaking a childhood infatuation that I had for you as love. I was only ten. I grew out of it. You're old enough to be my father."

"No!" screamed Michael. "If Father had not sent me off to Europe for six years, I would have seen the beautiful woman that you became. You would have fallen in love with me! But no! While I was gone, Jason took advantage of my absence! He stole you from me!"

"Michael, stop this!" screamed Jason. "She doesn't love you. She never did!"

"Liar!" Michael yelled. With that, he backhanded Jason, causing Jason to hit the ground.

"Jason!" Pauline cried in horror. She ran to her husband and got down next to him. She looked up at Michael, tears streaming down her cheeks.

"Leave us alone, you bastard!" she cried.

"Never, Pauline!" said Michael. "You are mine! And you and I are going to be together forever!"

Jason just stared up at his brother in disbelief, grasping his now injured jaw.

"You're insane, Michael!" exclaimed Jason. "Pauline and I are leaving! Now!"

They tried to get up off the floor, but Pauline began to feel lightheaded and dizzy. She looked at Jason and saw that he too was struggling to stand up. She felt as though time were slowing down around them. Pauline became weak and fell to the floor. She looked at Jason as he to fell down beside her. Pauline then looked up at Michael. He had a wicked smile plastered upon his face.

"Oh good," said Michael. "I'm glad that my little potion is starting to work. Rest well, you two."

As Pauline lay on the floor, her eyesight and hearing began to fade. At the moment, darkness began to consume her, and she became unconscious.

One hour later

"Wake up, love," whispered Michael in Pauline's ear. As she awoke, her eyes started to flutter.

"What-what happened?" she moaned. "Why is my heading aching?"

It was at that moment that she realized that she was lying on one of the sofas in the study. To her horror, she saw that her husband was unconscious and lying on the other sofa. His shirt had been ripped open, and strange symbols were painted all over his face and chest—in blood!

"Jason!" she screamed, as it was all coming back to her. She looked up at Michael.

"You monster!" she cried. "What have you done to him?"

"Don't worry, my love," said Michael. "That's not his blood. It's mine. I need to use my own blood for this to work."

"For what to work?" cried Pauline. Whatever he was talking about sent chills down her spine.

"Just a ritual in the dark arts that my mother taught me," he replied.

"Oh my God! It's true!" she cried in horror. "She was a witch!"

"Yes, my dear, and so am I," he replied. "And if there is one thing she taught me, it is that I can have anything I desire. That includes immortality—and you. See this dagger? It was my mother's, and it has been in her family for well over a millennium. It's made of silver. Do you know that some believed it was actually forged from the thirty pieces of silver that Judas received for betraying Jesus?"

"And if anyone would have it, it would be you!" she spat as she could feel tears welling up in her eyes.

Michael began to laugh.

"Unfortunately, my dear, I can neither confirm nor deny that claim," he said. "But you must admit that makes it quite the little conversation piece. Well, either way, Jason has become the lock. And the dagger is the key!"

"Oh my God! What do you mean?" she cried.

Michael just smiled at her.

"It's simple my dear," replied Michael. "He's going to be the blood sacrifice. Once I plunge this dagger into his heart, his soul will create an eternal void between life and death itself. The symbols that were drawn on him, in my blood, will allow my life-force to become one with the manor. I will then expel my brother's soul."

"You're mad!" cried Pauline. She jumped up off the sofa and ran toward her husband's unconscious body. She didn't know how, but she had to stop Michael from killing her husband.

Michael grabbed her as she came toward him. With his left arm wrapped around her body, he firmly held her wrists together with his right. She did her best to struggle but to no avail. She trembled in his arms as he stared at her with amorous lust.

"Don't worry, my dear," said Michael. "Being the good little boy that he's always been, I'm sure God will take favor upon him. Why would God be any different? I'm sure he loves Jason, just as everyone else does."

Michael's face had hardened as he talked of someone—yes, even God—loving Jason. But then his face softened, and he smiled at Pauline.

"Then you and I will be alone and together forever," he said, "and no one will ever take you away from me."

"Please don't!" she cried. "I'll do anything! I'll divorce Jason and marry you! Just don't kill him!"

"It's too late for that, my dear," he replied. "You should have accepted my marriage proposal a month ago. Besides, even if you're being honest now, I'm sure you would change your mind. It's better this way. Jason will be gone, and you and I will be somewhere no one will be able to find us. We will be together forever, both remaining eternally young, and your beauty will last forever."

He ran his hand down her cheek, but she turned her head away from him in disgust.

"Don't worry, my love," he said. "Eventually you will learn to crave my touch."

"Love!" she cried, in disgust. "What would a demon like you know about love?"

Michael's eyes darkened as he stared at her in anger.

"Perhaps you're right, my dear Pauline!" he exclaimed. "If that is the case, then you will have to be the one to teach me! Say goodbye to your husband!"

"*No!*" she screamed.

But it was too late. With great force and hatred in Michael's eyes, she watched him plunge the dagger into Jason's heart. To her horror, Jason's eyes popped open. He then let out one final gasp before he died.

Suddenly, colorful lightning began to move throughout the room. Michael grabbed her wrist and held it in a tight grip. She tried to get away, but he was too strong. She had to get out of there before it was too late.

Fortunately, when Michael wasn't paying attention, he had released his grasp on Pauline. He had made the mistake of turning his back on her. Pauline quickly removed the dagger from Jason's heart. And with determination, she plunged it into Michael's back and then pulled it out of him.

All of a sudden, Michael turned around to face her. With a shocked and angered expression upon his face, his eyes wide, he grabbed her forearm. She screamed and hastily jerked her arm away from him, releasing herself from Michael's grasp. With that, Michael let out one final gasp of air. He then collapsed dead on the floor.

Pauline, still crying, got down on the floor, reached into Michael's pocket, and grabbed the key. She stood up as fast as she could and ran to the locked door. Frantically, she tried to unlock the study door. She was trembling and had some trouble inserting the key into the lock. After her initial struggle, she was finally able to insert the key and unlock the door. She knew she had to get out of that house as soon as possible.

The house began to shake as Pauline entered the foyer. The walls were starting to crumble, and she felt cold wind blowing past her. She heard a loud creaking from above. She looked up and saw that the chandelier was starting to give way. Fortunately, she was able to get out of the way before it came crashing down upon the floor.

The huge mass of the finest European crystal exploded on the ground, right before her very eyes. Realizing how lucky she really was to still be alive, she ran toward the front door. But Michael's spirit appeared. She screamed as she saw his now ghostly apparition standing before her.

"You're not leaving, Pauline!" exclaimed Michael. "My corporeal form can be restored in the void, but I need a life-force to complete it! Since it can't be mine, it'll have to be yours! Pledge your eternal soul to me!"

"*Never!*" she cried.

"*Pauline!*" he yelled. "I own Jason's soul. If you don't pledge your eternal soul to me right now, his eternity will be an unbearable hell!" Before she could say anything, Jason's spirit also manifested just as Michael's had.

"Get away from her, you son of a bitch!" screamed Jason.

With what little energy he could muster, Jason pushed Michael out of the way, and Michael disappeared into the walls of the manor.

"Run, Pauline!" he cried. "Run, and don't look back at the manor! Please! I don't want you trapped here! Run! Run until you can't see this place anymore, and whatever you do, do not look into the manor!"

She could feel warm tears beginning to stream down her cheeks. She didn't want to leave him.

"I love you, Jason!" she cried.

Jason smiled at her with sorrow in his now ghostly eyes and ran his fingers down her cheeks. She closed her eyes and smiled as she felt cold fingers against her warm, teary face.

"*Pauline!*" Michael cried as his spirit reemerged in the foyer. "You're not leaving me!"

Pauline screamed in terror as she saw Michael's angered spirit staring back at them. At that moment, she was frozen in fear.

"Go!" screamed Jason. Her husband's cry gave her the strength to move. As much as she didn't want to leave him, she had no choice. She did what Jason told her and ran as far away as she could.

A terrible thunderstorm had begun as she ran across a now rain-soaked field. She didn't look back, but she heard what sounded like an explosion behind her. Between exhaustion and the tremors from the explosion, she collapsed to the ground crying.

She had gotten away, but Jason was trapped with that monster forever. She continued to scream and cry, as she knew she would never see her beloved Jason again.

"*Noooo!*" cried Pauline. "*Jasonnnn!*"

CHAPTER 1
A Deal with the Devil

Winworth Manor: Present Day

"That has got to be the dumbest excuse I have ever heard," said Robert.

Robert Gilmore kept shaking his head as he stared in disbelief at the massive eyesore in front of him. The entire manor was covered in moss and ivy. Some of the bricks that had fallen off the building were still lying on the ground as they had been for centuries.

It looked as though the entire home had been through a nuclear explosion, yet it was somehow still in one piece. Surprisingly, none of the windows had shattered. Every window in the building was still intact. However, they had somehow been mysteriously darkened. It was if the building itself was hiding a deep, dark secret.

"Well, that's why the town charter won't let it be torn down," replied his brother, Jonathan. "People believe that story to this day. They're afraid of that manor."

"Well, I would think they would want it torn down if that's the case. Aren't you the mayor?" asked Robert. "Can't you do something?"

"My hands are tied. It's not just the legend; it also has something to do with historical significance," said Jonathan. "Besides, to be honest with you, it really hasn't been a top priority of mine since Karen died only two months ago."

"I understand," said Robert. "Believe me, it's been hard on me since Helen died a few months ago. I think it's been twice as hard on Sarah. Speaking of Sarah, where did she go?"

The young girl, Sarah, Robert's daughter, had just turned sixteen. She had emerald-green eyes and long, wavy, luxurious red hair. She was at that age when not only boys but young men were starting to notice her.

Robert didn't know how to handle the situation. His little girl had practically become a woman overnight. She needed her mother, but his beloved Helen had been taken from them.

As he looked around, to his relief, he saw her standing in front of the home. She just kept intensely staring at it. Something had caught her attention.

***

Entranced by the display in front of her. Sarah stared in wonder at the decaying yet once immaculate manor.

"Daddy, is that it?" she asked. "Why do you want to tear it down? I think it's amazing! I can just picture it in its heyday. I want to live there." She stared at it in amazement and closed her eyes. She could easily envision what it must have once looked like. She imagined a grand ballroom.

The floor was made out of marbled tile. Most of it was ivory, with a red marbled sunburst in the center of the dance floor. The giant windows were adorned with thick dark-red velvet curtains. A few portraits hung along the ivory-colored walls, and the entire room was lit up by three massive brass chandeliers. This gave the room a warm, romantic glow.

"Sweetheart," he replied, "I'm sure at one time it was a beautiful home, but it hasn't been taken care of in almost two hundred years. It's dilapidated beyond repair."

Sarah wasn't paying any attention to her father. She was just too enamored with the vision of what the manor once looked like. Just then, she could feel a cold breeze whirling around her body. It was at that moment that she heard a man's voice inside her mind.

"Who are you, my titan-haired angel?" the provocative husky voice asked her. *"At last, I've found you! You're the one I've been searching for all this time! Soon, my pretty one, you will be mine!"*

The voice enchanted her, like a lover calling out to her; she was under its seductive spell. It was drawing her into its hypnotic embrace. Without even realizing it, she started walking toward the manor. As she did, the world around her seemed to be fading into nothingness.

"Sarah? Sarah, stop! Don't go in there!" cried her father. She felt her father grab her, and it snapped her back into reality. She felt a little dizzy and had no idea why this was happening to her.

"I'm sorry, Daddy," she replied. "I don't know what came over me. For some reason, I'm just drawn to it."

"Well, just get back in the car, and we'll head to Jonathan's," he told her.

***

As she made her way back to the car, Jonathan was horrified. It was at that moment that he realized what was happening to Sarah.

Damn it, Robert! he thought. *Oh my God! Why didn't you tell me? Shit! I didn't know that she had blossomed so quickly. I was used to her being an awkward little girl, but she's become a beautiful young woman. If I had known any of this, I would have met you guys at my place first. I never would have let you bring her here! She has to leave now—before it's too late!*

"Robert, take Sarah, and get the hell out of this town!" cried Jonathan.

Robert just stared at his brother in total disbelief.

"What the hell, Jonathan?" Robert asked in confusion.

"Listen to me, Robert," Jonathan explained. "Sarah isn't safe here. If I tried to explain it, you wouldn't believe me. Just trust me, if you stay here, Sarah will be in danger."

"Jonathan!" yelled Robert. "What the hell's your problem? I'm beginning to think you're as nutty as the rest of this town."

"Look Rob—" Jonathan began.

However, the manor began to shake, causing him to look back at it in terror.

"What was that?" asked Robert.

"Um, it … it's just the old place settling," said Jonathan. He then heard Michael's angry voice inside his head. Out of fear and sorrow, Jonathan slowly began to close his eyes.

"Jonathan!" Michael shouted. *"We had an agreement!"*

Jonathan then opened his eyes and looked at his brother.

"You know what, Robert," Jonathan began. "I'm … I'm sorry. It's just that I feel overprotective of my family since Karen died. I guess I haven't seen you guys in a long time, and I'd forgotten how much Sarah had probably grown. I guess I was worried about some of the men who might be tempted by the new pretty face in town. I-I suppose I was overreacting. Don't get me wrong; this is a nice town. It's just that Sarah looks older than sixteen. Some men might be temped to take advantage of her naïveté."

"Look, Jonathan, thanks for being concerned," said Robert. "But I am her father. I will keep an eye on her. Believe me, I've had to scare off a few young men back home. I think I can handle them out here as well."

"You're right, Robert. I'm … I'm sorry," said Jonathan. "Here are the keys to my house. Why don't you take Sarah there, and you guys can get settled. I'll be along in a little while. I just have some business to finish up here."

"Okay then, Sarah and I will see you in a little bit," replied Robert. With that, he got in the car, and he and Sarah left for his brother's house. As they drove off, Jonathan turned around and looked back toward the manor.

"Please, not her!" Jonathan cried. "She's my niece, and she's only sixteen."

"In my day, sixteen was a full-grown woman," Michael replied. *"If you didn't want me to choose her, then why did you bring her before me?"*

"I-I didn't know she had practically blossomed overnight," Jonathan explained. "Please, they too have suffered a recent tragedy. My brother's wife, the girl's mother, she was killed a few months ago. Please, I'm begging you—don't do this. You've already taken too much from me. Don't take my niece away from her father."

"It's too late, Jonathan!" exclaimed Michael. *"We have stared into each other's souls. I have fallen in love. She is the one I want. You promised to find me a bride. You will not interfere! If you do, the deal is off, and Karen's soul will be trapped here forever. Do you really want your beloved wife to spend eternity as a mere chambermaid?"*

"Why did you have to kill her?" asked Jonathan.

"I had no choice but to kill her," Michael explained. *"She was conspiring with your brother to have me destroyed. Anyone who tries to demolish me has to be punished. I take their souls, and then they serve me."*

"What do you mean by serve you?" asked Jonathan. "Please tell me you didn't touch her!"

"As tempting as it may be—after all, Karen was a beautiful woman—I have not laid a hand on your wife," explained Michael. *"Not only is that*

something I am saving for my bride-to-be, but I can only have relations with a living being. I can only experience sexual pleasure though a living being's own sexual gratification. It would be pointless for two spirits to even try."

"Why do you feel the need to imprison so many souls?" cried Jonathan.

"Because the more souls I collect, the more powerful I become," Michael replied. *"The energy from their souls makes the manor more powerful. My spirit is connected to the manor. So inside the manor is where I am practically my own deity."*

"Oh my God!" cried Jonathan.

"Not quite, Jonathan!" Michael exclaimed in annoyance. *"Now, if I may continue? Even though my powers weaken the further I go, I can actually leave the manor. But my spirit can only travel within a certain perimeter. Fortunately, your home is within that perimeter. That means I can visit my beloved Sarah before she is brought to me."*

"What does that mean?" asked Jonathan.

"That is none of your concern!" said Michael.

"Look! There's a girls' college in the neighboring town," said Jonathan. "I've talked to the history department. Many beautiful young women will be visiting next week to learn more about the manor's historical significance. They will also be viewing the manor's exterior structure from a safe distance. But they will be close enough to the manor for you to observe them. I'm sure you would find a girl you'd like even better than Sarah."

"Sarah is the one I love. She is the one I want, and she is the one I shall have!" Michael replied. *"Besides, the manor won't be here next week. Once the manor is restored, and the void is completed, my beautiful angel and I will depart this world. She and I will create our eternal paradise, one in which no one will ever be able to find us or come between us. It will be our own special heaven, one in which I am God!"*

"You are an insane, egotistical megalomaniac!" Jonathan spat.

"Do not test my patience, Jonathan!" growled Michael, *"Remember, I own Karen's soul! Now you wouldn't want her to pay for your own disrespectful behavior, would you? Also, I know that it was your brother, as well as Karen, who was planning on having me destroyed. The only reason I didn't kill him as soon as he came to the manor is because of my love for Sarah. I will probably have to use him to get her to agree to marry me."*

"Please!" cried Jonathan. "Don't kill my brother!"

"*Don't worry, Jonathan,*" replied Michael. "*As long as Sarah agrees to be mine for all eternity, there will be no reason for me to harm him. My guess is that she will be a good girl and be very cooperative.*"

"Sarah loves her father more than anything," cried Jonathan. "She would never let him die."

"*Good, my perfect little selfless angel,*" said Michael. "*You know, after I took Karen's life, I had my intuition that you were the key to finding my chosen bride. I had assumed it was because of your status in this meaningless town. But now I see that it was because my future bride-to-be was a blood relative of yours. I guess she gets most her traits from the material side of her ancestry.*"

Jonathan closed his eyes and did all that he could to hold back his tears.

"*There's no need to cry, Jonathan,*" said Michael. "*Just think—once I marry Sarah, Karen's soul will go free. Then Sarah and I will live happily ever after for all eternity. Everybody wins. Surely you can't have a problem with that?*"

Jonathan continued to keep his closed eyes; he felt completely numb.

"No," he replied, "I suppose not."

"*I'm glad we agree,*" said Michael. "*Oh, and one other thing. If any man so much as tries to lay a finger on her, he too will be punished. Do you understand?*"

"Yes," replied Jonathan.

"*Good. Then if I were you, I'd keep an eye on her,*" ordered Michael. "*As you told your brother earlier, some men might not act appropriately toward the new pretty face in town. If they don't, well, the manor can always use more servants. Now then, I think you'd better head home. You don't want to keep your brother and niece waiting.*"

***

Jonathan did as Michael commanded and got in his car. Before starting the ignition, he took out his wallet and removed a picture of his beloved Karen. He began to cry as he gently traced her beautiful image in the photo. He looked at her long brown hair as it shone in the sunlight, the smile from her ruby lips that could easily brighten the darkness, and her eyes—those chocolate-brown doe eyes were staring back at him. They were staring into his soul.

"Please forgive me, Karen!" he cried. "I'm sorry I didn't protect you. I'm sorry that bastard killed you! But most of all, please forgive me for what I'm about to do. I don't have a choice. It's either you or Sarah. I love Sarah, but I love you more. I would do anything for you, even if that means I have to betray my own brother and our own goddaughter." He watched as his tears began to fall on her picture. Jonathan then took out a handkerchief from his breast pocket and wiped it off before the picture could be damaged. He continued to look at the image of his beloved wife.

"But Michael won't hurt Sarah," he continued. "I promise. I swear, Karen, I wouldn't agree to it if I thought he would. If anything, he will love her and bestow upon her his complete and utter adoration and devotion. Besides, even if I refuse him, he'll have her no matter what. He takes whatever he wants, and what he wants is Sarah. At least if I help him, he'll let you go. Please understand why I must do this. I love you, Karen!"

Jonathan then composed himself and wiped away his tears. He kissed the picture, put it back into his wallet, started the car, and drove away.

***

"Jonathan, don't do this!" a desperate voice cried out to him. But she knew it was all in vain. She watched her husband drive away, unable to hear her cries. Even though she knew she could incur her captor's wrath, she had to try—she had to plead with him not to take Sarah. She knew he would be angry at her going to him without being summoned. But she felt as though she didn't have any other choice.

"Michael!" cried Karen. "Please don't do this!" Her ghostly eyes widened in terror as she saw malevolent anger in Michael's reaction upon seeing her.

"Shut up, woman!" cried Michael's angry spirit. "Why are you here before me? I do not recall summoning you! Why were you eavesdropping? Answer me!"

"They're my family!" she cried. "I have to make sure you don't hurt them!"

***

Michael began to seethe with rage. How dare she be so disrespectful toward him? *Does she honestly believe that she is still someone of importance?*

"Learn your place, Karen!" Michael exclaimed. "How many times must I tell you? You might have once been first lady of this meaningless town, but now you are just a glorified housekeeper at best!"

"Please I—" she started to beg, but he interrupted her.

"Silence!" screamed Michael. "You have angered me, and now you have to be punished! Since you're a woman, even a spirit of a woman, I will not inflict pain upon you. I am too much a gentleman to do that. However, you may watch as I inflict pain on my brother in your place!"

"No, please don't!" she cried.

"Jason!" Michael demanded.

***

Jason's spirit appeared before them. He saw the sorrow and fear in Karen's expression. Whatever wrong Michael thought Karen had done, Jason knew that he was the one who was going to pay for it. Jason looked toward Karen.

"It's going to be all right," he mouthed, trying to reassure her. He then shot her a quick wink.

Michael just laughed at them.

"Believe me, Jason," said Michael. "It's not going to be all right, not for you."

Michael then looked at Karen with angry malevolence in his eyes.

"Jason's suffering will be because of you, my dear!" yelled Michael. "And you will watch me torture him! Just keep in mind as you watch him suffer that it is all your fault!"

***

CHAPTER 2
The Master and His Servants

Karen watched in horror as Michael inflicted pain upon Jason in her place.

"Please, Michael, stop!" she cried. "He doesn't deserve this!"

"What did you call me?" Michael screamed, looking at her with rage.

All Michael had to do was close his eyes, and Jason felt as though he had an actual body that was on fire. It was as if Jason's ghostly form had real flesh melting off of it. The more Jason screamed in pain and begged for mercy, the more Michael laughed sadistically.

"Please, Lord Winworth," she pleaded. "Please just stop hurting him."

Michael turned to look at her and saw the sadness in her eyes. He released Jason from his torture. He then walked over to his broken brother.

"My, my, Brother!" Michael chuckled. "What do we have here? Are you two starting to develop feelings for one another? First, you stole Pauline from me, and now you're trying to steal Mayor Gilmore's wife. What is it with you and this chambermaid? Some sort of Oedipus complex? And everyone thought I was the bad one."

"You're a son of bitch!" Jason spat. He was slowly recovering from his brother's torture.

"Yes, I know," Michael replied. "Well, at least that's what I heard, but in her case, she was actually a witch."

"She was evil, just like you!" Jason screamed.

"Maybe," Michael responded, "but at least my mother wasn't a cheap little gold-digging whore, unlike yours."

"My mother loved our father!" Jason cried. "He fell in love with her on his own. Your mother was a witch, who cast a spell on him! It was Elizabeth who was the gold-digging whore!"

9

"Liar!" Michael screamed. "Don't ever speak my mother's name again! My parents were happily married until that French slut, a mere chambermaid, seduced him. She then became pregnant with you, a repugnant parasite growing within her womb. You! You were her assurance to my family's wealth! She used her seductive hold over our father to impregnate her. Then she convinced to him to murder my mother!"

"No!" cried Jason. "Lie to yourself, Michael! But do not lie to me! My mother loved our father. Your mother married Father for his wealth, not his love. She did not even know how to love anyone, not even you."

"I don't know what you are talking about!" screamed Michael. "My mother loved me. That's why she taught me everything about dark magic!"

"Maybe when you were a small child, she had some affection toward you," said Jason. "But as you got older, she grew to hate you. She didn't like the fact that Father loved you. She was jealous of you, her own child! A loving mother doesn't rape her own son! That's why father killed her, to save you!"

"Shut up, you worthless little bastard!" screamed Michael. "Did that bitch, your mother, tell you that?"

"My mother didn't say anything to me about it!" Jason screamed. "Our father told me! You know why? He warned me to always stay on guard around you. Obviously, I did not listen, or I wouldn't be here right now. He said if anything strange happened to him, or my mother, you would likely be the culprit."

"I know he always favored you, Jason, his prodigal son," Michael replied in a sarcastic but calmer tone. "You know, after your mother and our dear father were killed in that untimely carriage accident, no one ever figured out what exactly spooked the horses."

"You bastard!" screamed Jason. "I knew you killed them!"

"Oh my God!" cried Karen. She had a look upon her face of both horror and disbelief.

Michael let out a maniacal laugh as he turned his attention toward her.

"Aren't you enjoying yourself, my dear?" Michael asked. "You should feel honored. There are very few who get to learn about all the skeletons in the Winworth family closet."

Karen said nothing; she was too dumbfounded to even respond. Dark, malevolent anger appeared in Michael's eyes.

"I asked you a question, Karen!" yelled Michael.

"She does not have to respond, Michael!" exclaimed Jason.

"Oh! She doesn't have to respond, does she?" asked Michael sarcastically. "Is that so, Jason? You know, I wasn't really being serious about the possibility of a relationship between the two of you. But now, I am starting think maybe there really is something there."

"We are just friends, Michael," replied Jason. "Our friendship is the only thing that helps get us through this hellish existence that has become our prison."

"Don't feel the need to be shy, Jason." Michael laughed. "No one would blame you if you had developed feelings for her. After all, she is quite lovely, even in spirited form."

Michael looked at Karen with undeniable lust in his eyes. Yet it was lust he never seemed to want to act upon, nor did he ever try. Yet he flashed a genuine smile toward her.

"Get to whatever point you are trying to make, Michael!" demanded Jason.

"The point is, dear brother," replied Michael as he turned toward Jason, "the irony of all of this. See, I just realized, at this very moment, that I didn't really love Pauline. I mistook a combination of being enchanted by her classic beauty and my hatred toward you as love. But you already knew that, didn't you?"

Jason became infuriated.

"So you're telling me that this was all for nothing?" cried Jason. "That the last two hundred years of my hellish existence and separating me from my wife was all a mistake?"

"No," replied Michael. "In fact, quite the contrary. If none of that had ever happened, then I never would have met my beautiful Sarah. We never would have stared into one another's soul. Like Karen, so many beautiful women passed by the manor. Sarah was the only one for whom I felt true, unconditional love. Tell me, Brother—is this wonderful feeling that I have toward Sarah, similar to what you felt toward Pauline?"

"What do you think, Michael?" replied Jason.

"Hmm," said Michael, "I think I feel sorry for what I did to you, Jason ... well, almost."

"Go to hell, Michael!" cried Jason.

"I will not be disrespected in my own home!" exclaimed Michael. "I am the lord of the manor. And when Sarah becomes my eternal bride, she shall become the lady of the manor. You, Jason, and the rest of those imprisoned here shall be our servants. After all, as the lord and lady of the manor, Sarah and I will need obedient servants—except for you, Karen. If your husband delivers Sarah to me, as I have instructed him, your soul goes free."

"I don't want my freedom at the cost of Sarah's!" Karen cried.

"Sarah is going to be happy and in love with me!" screamed Michael. "Learn your place, woman! How many times must I warn you! Jason, what I'm about to do to you will be all Karen's fault!"

"*No!*" screamed Karen in horror. She couldn't even look at the terrible treatment Jason was receiving. Karen kept hearing his cries of agony. All she could think about was how it was all her fault. Deep down, she knew it was actually Michael's fault, but that gave her little comfort in the situation unfolding right in front of her.

Michael had tortured Jason many times, even just for fun. But when he was acting out of anger, the pain that Michael inflicted upon him was unimaginable.

***

Chapter 3
Familial Relations

Robert and Sarah arrived at Jonathan's house. As they got out of the car, Sarah still couldn't get the image of the manor out of her head. Why was she so obsessed with it?

She just kept picturing what it must have looked like when it was still in all its magnificent glory. She closed her eyes, and a sudden chill entered the air. Sarah started to feel like she was falling into some form of trance. She heard multiple voices that sounded like distant echoes. However, the echoes were inside her own head.

"Sarah! Sarah! Sarah!" a symphony of voices echoed in her mind. However, they were soon replaced by a sensual, haunting male voice. It was the same one that she had heard earlier, when she looked into the manor.

"Come to me, Sarah! Come to me!" his voice called to her. *"Come to me, my love, and be mine forever!"*

The voice startled her and quickly brought her out of the spell she was under. She let out a loud gasp and looked around, but no one was there.

"Are you all right, Sarah?" her father asked.

"Do you hear that?" she asked him.

"Hear what?" he responded.

"I thought I heard a man's voice," she replied.

"Yeah, it was me asking you to get your bag out of the car," he said, and he smiled at her. "You know, while you were daydreaming?"

"No," she replied with confusion. "It got cold all of a sudden, and then I heard it."

"Honey, it's ninety degrees out here," he replied. "I wish there was a chill in the air. I think you were just in the car too long. You're probably tired. You have seemed out of it since we got here. You scared the hell out of me when you almost walked into that death trap earlier."

"I'm sorry, Daddy," she told him. "Maybe I am tired. I think I'm just hearing things."

"It's okay, princess. I'll forgive you … this time," he said with a smile. He wrapped his arms around her and pulled her into a loving embrace. She smiled back as he gave her a quick peck on the forehead.

"I'm glad I have you, Daddy," she said. "I love you so much, and I miss Mom. It's not fair. Why did she have to die?"

"Oh, sweetheart, I don't know the answer," he responded. "But I do know one thing: I couldn't have gotten through this nightmare without you. I don't know what I would have done if you hadn't been in my life. The older you get, the more you look and act like your mother. That is the highest compliment I could ever pay a person. Just promise me that you'll always remember how much I love you."

"I will, Daddy," she replied and smiled back at him. She gave him a quick peck on the cheek.

As they started to head toward the entrance of the house, they saw a familiar face.

"Oh my God!" the young man exclaimed. "Is that Sarah?"

"Todd Miller, as I live and breathe!" Robert replied, giving him a quick hug. "Sarah, you remember Todd, Karen's brother."

"Um, maybe a little," she replied. Sarah flashed a mischievous smile. The brown-haired, blue-eyed young man that she remembered from her youth stood before her. She had always thought he was cute. But now, as an older man, she found him quite handsome.

"Oh, I know you remember me," he said. "You used to kick me all time."

"That's 'cause I liked you," she said, giggling.

"Well, if I knew you were going to turn out like this, I might have let you kick me more often," he responded.

Sarah began to blush. She always did like older men.

"Keep in mind she's only sixteen, Todd," they heard a voice say. "You're thirty."

They turned around and saw Jonathan as he started getting out of his car.

"Oh, lighten up, Jonathan," said Robert. "They're not being serious. It's just cordial banter."

"What are you doing here anyway, Todd?" asked Jonathan.

"I knew they were coming by today," said Todd. "It's been at least eleven years. I just wanted to stop by, see them, and pay my respects about Helen. I was heartbroken when Karen called and told me she had died.

"Well, you should have called here first," Jonathan sneered. In reality, Jonathan feared for Todd's life. He was afraid that Michael would kill Todd if he showed any signs of interest in Sarah.

The four of them then went inside the house. As they entered through the front door, Robert turned to Todd.

"I'm worried about Jonathan," Robert whispered. "He just doesn't seem the same. I suppose it's understandable, considering Karen's sudden death. By the way, how are you holding up these days?"

"It's been difficult," Todd replied. "Especially what happened. I still don't get it. How does a woman of thirty-eight die of a heart attack? You are right about Jonathan though; he just hasn't been the same."

"Excuse me, Todd," Jonathan began. "I need to talk to my brother for just a second."

"Sure, no problem," he said. "I'll just hang out with Sarah."

"Actually, Todd, I think it would be better if you just left right now," Jonathan spat.

Both Robert and Todd looked at Jonathan in disbelief.

Feeling hurt and angry, Todd threw his hands up in the air.

"Look, if you don't want me here, I'll just leave," he said. "I don't want to be a problem." Obviously annoyed, he started to walk toward the front door.

"Todd, wait!" cried Robert, but he didn't respond.

"You were being a bit rude, Jonathan, don't you think?" asked Robert.

"Look, Robert," Jonathan began. "I just think it would be best if he stayed away from Sarah. I mean, she's only sixteen, and he's thirty. He's way too old for her. I would think as her father you would be careful of things like that."

"Jonathan, are you accusing me of being a bad parent?" asked Robert.

"No, of course not," said Jonathan. "It's just you haven't seen Todd in eleven years. Look, he's my brother-in-law. I love him. It's just that he gets around a lot. I'm just afraid he might forget her age and try something. Keep him away from her, just to be safe. Please, I know I was rude. I'm sorry. I offended both him and you. It's just been so hard since I lost Karen. You have to forgive me if I don't seem like myself anymore."

"It's okay, Jonathan," said Robert. "Believe me, no one understands more than me. But I think it's Todd who really deserves your apology."

"You're right," said Jonathan. "I-I will, of course, I will apologize to him. I just want to keep all my loved ones safe. I couldn't handle anyone being hurt right now. Just promise me that you'll keep her out of situations she may be too naive to handle."

"She's my daughter. I'll protect her, Jonathan," replied Robert. "You don't have to worry about her well-being."

"Just keep her away from Todd, okay?" said Jonathan.

"If that's what you want," replied Robert. "I still think he's a nice young man, but you know him better than I do."

"Good," Jonathan said and smiled. "Tell you what. Once you and Sarah settle in, the three of us will grab a bite to eat. My treat."

"Sounds great," replied Robert, smiling back at him.

He began to head upstairs. Sarah was waiting for him at the top of the stairs.

"Is Uncle Jon okay?" she asked.

Her father placed his hands on her forearms. He sighed and looked at her with a sad expression.

"No, sweetheart, he's not."

***

Chapter 4
A Dark Temptation

It was about ten o'clock the very next morning. Jonathan made his way down to the kitchen. He was still in his pajamas, looking tired and disheveled. He found his brother already dressed and helping himself to a cup of coffee.

"Good morning," yawned Jonathan. "I would ask you how you slept, but it looks like you slept pretty well."

"I did sleep pretty well," replied Robert. "I was so tired from traveling yesterday, I fell asleep as soon as my head hit the pillow. I hope you don't mind, I went ahead and brewed a pot of coffee. Would you like some?"

"Thanks," said Jonathan. "I think I will have a cup of coffee, black."

"Black? It sounds like you didn't sleep too well last night if you want it that strong," said Robert, and he poured Jonathan's coffee.

"Actually, I haven't had a good night's sleep in the past couple of months," said Jonathan. "Things have just been crazy around here. Karen and I moved to the Long Island shoreline so we could have more tranquility in our lives. We had been here for five years, and we were so happy. Then, just like that, she was gone."

"Jonathan, why didn't you want Sarah and me to come to the funeral?" asked Robert.

Jonathan took another sip of his coffee.

"Because half the people in this town are crazy," Jonathan began. "They believe the legend about that manor. A lot of people think that the ghost of Michael Winworth killed Karen."

"What? Why?" asked Robert.

"Because she was trying to work with you to have the manor torn down," Jonathan responded. "It seems that anytime that manor has a possibility of being demolished, the one trying to tear it down dies of a heart attack. I was afraid that if you came here, so soon after her death, half the town would have been upset. Everyone knew that you were working with Karen on the resort project. I was afraid some might harass you. People are afraid of that place."

Robert just shook his head in total disbelief.

"People really believe that?" asked Robert. "Why would they not want me here? It would have been my life in danger, if they actually believed that nonsense."

"Yes. But it is also believed that if Michael stops a person's heart, their soul is trapped in the manor," Jonathan replied. "The more souls he collects, the more powerful he becomes."

"That's crazy," said Robert. "This is the twenty-first century. Are people really that superstitious around here?"

"I'm afraid so," said Jonathan, as he looked around. "By the way, is Sarah still asleep?"

"No. She wanted to go for a walk. She left an hour ago," replied Robert.

Jonathan's eyes widened as his heart almost skipped a beat.

"You let her just wander out there by herself?" asked Jonathan. "I mean, she doesn't know her way around here."

Robert looked surprised by his brother's reaction.

"She's sixteen, not six. I doubt she'll get lost," said Robert. "Besides, it's mid-morning. I think she'll be safe. I wouldn't let her go if it was night."

She may be safe, thought Jonathan. *But any man who shows an interest in her won't be.*

"You know what, Robert? I have some things to do downtown today," said Jonathan. "If I run into Sarah, maybe-maybe I'll give her a lift home."

"Um, okay, if you want. I doubt that'll be necessary," said Robert. "Sarah has her phone. I'll call her later to check up on her. I'm meeting with the land developer today. We're going to check out some available properties further down the shore. Hopefully, this resort project isn't dead. I have a lot of investors lined up. They're not going to be too happy with me if this deal falls through."

Robert sighed. Being an independent real estate contractor could be risky. If he worked for a real estate company, taking such a loss would be bad, but it wouldn't completely destroy him. If the deal were to fall through, he could lose everything. He already had so much of his personal assets invested in it.

***

Sarah was walking along the beach, enjoying the scent of the fresh sea air. She had always loved the beach. With her eyes closed, she felt the warmth of the sun and the gentle breeze against her skin. The sounds of the ocean and the seagulls stirred such happy memories.

Some of her fondest memories were of the beach vacations. It was always a special time that she spent with her mother and father. The three of them would laugh as they walked along the shore, the waves crashing into them along the way. It made her a little sad. She was starting to miss her mother.

Her uncle's home was located on the shore, so she just kept walking along the beach. Eventually, she came upon a chain-link fence that completely blocked off a beachfront property. It was the manor. For some odd reason, she felt the need to see it one more time.

She made her way up to the street and just stared at it. The manor was damaged well beyond repair, but for some reason, she could see the beauty of its structure. She could look beyond its current state and imagine what it once had been. The more she stared at it, the more she became entranced. She felt another chill in the air as a cold wind came out of nowhere.

"Sarah!" the haunting male voice called to her. *"Come to me, Sarah! You belong here with me. You are mine—and only mine—to love. You belong to me and only me. Come to me, and I will love you forever."*

Once again, the voice enchanted her. It was almost hypnotic. Without even realizing it, she started to walk toward the dilapidated building.

"Hey!" a cheery voice cried.

To Sarah's surprise, Todd just seemed to come out of nowhere. Startled, she snapped out of the trance. She jumped and then let out a loud gasp.

"Oh my God!" she exclaimed. "You scared me!"

"I'm sorry, Sarah, I didn't mean to frighten you," said Todd.

"That's okay, Todd. I'll forgive you … *this* time," she quipped. "How did you know I was here?"

"I was driving over to Jonathan's," he replied. "I wanted to apologize for intruding. I didn't mean to upset him yesterday. Well, anyway, I saw you when I was driving by here. You know, it's kind of hard to miss that bright-red hair. So what are you doing out here anyway? Were-were you about to walk in there?"

"It's so weird," she replied. "I'm just drawn to it. I didn't realize that I was starting to walk inside. It's so strange. I didn't even hear you drive up."

"Well, then I'm glad I found you when I did," he said. "Legend has it that if you go in there, you never come out."

"You don't really believe that?" asked Sarah.

"No," he replied. "But I bet there's a good chance part of the ceiling could fall on your head. You hungry?"

"Starving," she responded with a smile.

"Well, come on. I'll take you to the best burger joint in town," Todd told her, returning her smile. He put his arm around her and walked her to his car.

***

Michael's spirit had continued watching as they got into Todd's car and drove away. He was livid. She was almost in his grasp. But what really angered Michael was that a filthy Neanderthal had put his arm around Sarah—*his* Sarah! He knew that killing Todd would upset her. As angry as he was, upsetting her was the last thing he wanted to do.

"Damn it!" he yelled. "She was coming to me. She was going to be mine!"

He let himself calm down a bit, but he was going to have to keep an eye on them.

"Don't worry, my beautiful angel," he said. "You will soon be with me for all eternity. No man could ever love you as much as I do. I will make you feel bodily pleasures that no other man could ever make you feel. But if any other man tries, he'll die a horrible death. That, I guarantee."

***

Karen had heard Michael's anger directed toward her brother. Out of sheer desperation, she and Jason manifested themselves within Michael's presence.

"Please, don't hurt my brother, Todd!" begged Karen. "He won't try anything, I swear."

"I don't care who the hell he is, Karen!" screamed Michael. "If he tries anything with her, any way of trying to entice her, he's dead! And your worthless husband will be the one to blame. I told him to keep an eye on her. If Todd has to die, his blood will be on Jonathan's hands."

***

CHAPTER 5
Forbidden Fruit

Todd and Sarah made their way into the restaurant. Both ordered the combo special, a double cheeseburger, fries, and a soft drink.

As they were waiting for their food, her father called. She told him how she had run into Todd. She promised that after they finished their lunch, Todd would bring her straight home.

"So what makes this the best burger joint in town?" Sarah asked Todd.

"Well," Todd began, "there are many factors to consider. First, there's the quality of the food, then price value, restaurant cleanliness, how friendly the service is … and then there's the one factor that's the most important of all."

"Oh yeah, what's that?" she asked, with a flirty smile.

"There's also the fact that this is the only burger joint in town," he replied.

She looked at him and just laughed.

"Yeah, I think this is the only American town that doesn't have a McDonald's in it," she said. "So do you like living in New York? I haven't seen you since you moved away."

"Oh, I love it," he replied. "It's big though, much bigger than Indianapolis. You could live in New York your whole life, and you still wouldn't be able to experience everything that there is to do there."

"Wow!" she replied. "That does sound like an exciting place to live. I'd like to visit New York City someday. To get here yesterday, we drove a route that went around the city limits. But you could still see it. I had never seen such a massive place before, I couldn't believe it. Daddy said that if we have time, we might take the train into Manhattan. I really would like to visit the Big Apple."

"You should, Sarah," said Todd. "You'd love it. Maybe when you're older, um, *much* older, you could visit, and I'll show you around."

"Okay, it's a date," replied Sarah. "So have you been here since Aunt Karen's funeral?"

"Pretty much," he replied. "When she died, I took a three-month sabbatical from work. I was hoping to help Jonathan cope with the situation. It hit both of us pretty hard, but he's just been so distant. He's not the same person. After what happened yesterday, I think maybe it would be best if I just go back to work. I'm not really helping him, and I can't really put my life on hold anymore."

"I know Daddy's really worried about him," she said. "I mean Daddy was devastated by my mom's death but not like Uncle Jon. Aunt Karen's death hit him pretty hard."

"Well, you also have to keep in mind that your father has you," he told her. "Jonathan and Karen never had children. He doesn't have the support your father has. How are you coping with your mother's death?"

"It's been really hard on me," she replied. "I really need my mom right now. I have so many questions that I just can't ask Daddy. I know girls who are younger than me and have a lot more experience. I mean, I've never even kissed a guy."

"I find that hard to believe," said Todd. "I have to be honest with you, Sarah, a part of me wishes you were five years older. But don't tell your dad that. I think he would kill me."

Sarah's eyes became as wide as saucers. She then gave him a shy smile and began to blush.

I wish I was five years older too! she thought.

"It'll be our little secret," she said.

***

God, she's so cute when she's nervous, thought Todd. *Dear Lord! What am I thinking? She's only sixteen, Todd! Get ahold of yourself. Plus, she's my sister's niece. If Karen were alive, she'd kill me if she knew what I was thinking about right now!*

"Anyway," began Todd, "you can't believe everything the kids at school tell you. Half the stuff they brag about is usually exaggerated. Besides, there's nothing wrong with waiting for first-time experiences. I know this is going to sound like a cliché, but that doesn't make it any less true. All first-time experiences are better when they're special."

"I know," she replied. "But thanks for caring enough to remind me."

"You're welcome, my lady," Todd replied as he playfully smiled and bowed his head.

This made Sarah chuckle, and she blushed.

"So how have you been holding up through all of this?" she asked.

"Well, okay, considering," he replied. "It just destroyed my parents. They saw a therapist, and he suggested they just get away for a while. They just started a thirty-day European cruise a couple of days ago. I hope it helps. What's really been hard is dealing with some of the nutjobs in this town."

"What do you mean?" she asked.

"I mean people that I don't even know, some of the weird things they've come up and said to me," he told her.

"Like what?" she asked.

"Like they think that an evil spirit killed my sister, out of spite," he replied, "because she was trying to have the manor torn down. It was her dream to own a hotel on the beach. The manor seemed like the perfect spot for it. After Jonathan was elected mayor, things started to move forward. That's when they brought your father on board. Then, all of a sudden, she drops dead from a heart attack. Just like that. She was a thirty-eight-year-old woman. Do you have any idea how rare that is?"

"No, but I know it's not common," said Sarah. "Things have been so crazy this past year. I don't think anything could surprise me anymore."

***

As they finished eating, Sarah couldn't help but notice a middle-aged woman who just kept staring at her. The woman was dressed in a new-age bohemian-style outfit. Sarah felt uncomfortable as the strange woman's eyes were practically shooting daggers toward her.

Why does this crazy old hippie keep staring at me? wondered Sarah.

"Earth to Sarah," cried Todd. "What has your mind preoccupied this time?"

"Oh nothing," replied Sarah. "Some creepy woman keeps staring at me."

Casually, Todd turned around to look. He immediately knew which woman Sarah was referencing.

"Oh her," replied Todd. "I can't remember her name right now. But you know how I said this town was full of nutjobs?"

"Yes," replied Sarah.

"Well, that's their queen," he said.

Sarah just laughed.

"You're terrible, Todd!" she told him.

After they finished their lunch, Todd threw a twenty on the table to pay for the food. Sarah noticed the same crazy woman was still watching her as they left the restaurant. The woman gave Sarah the creeps, but she just decided to ignore her.

As they walked outside, they headed for Todd's car. Since it was a nice day, they walked through the park that was in the middle of town. Sarah really loved how quaint the seaside town really was. There were so many neat little shops and trendy places to eat. No wonder her aunt had wanted to build a resort here.

"This is a great little town," said Sarah. "I wish my mom could have seen it. I feel so guilty."

Todd just furrowed his brow as he looked at Sarah.

"Why would you feel guilty?" he asked.

"The night before my Mom died ..." she began.

***

The Gilmore Household
Indianapolis, Six Months Ago ...

It was five minutes after ten on a Saturday night. Sarah had been out with her friends and had just walked through the front door.

"Sarah Jane Gilmore!" cried her mother, Helen. "Your curfew was ten o'clock! You are five minutes late!"

"Oh come on, Mom!" cried Sarah. "It was just five lousy minutes! Are you really going to get this upset over that?"

"When I say ten o'clock, I mean ten o'clock!" replied her mother.

"But, Mom," cried Sarah, "all my friends have eleven o'clock curfews. Look, I'm sorry that I'm a little late, but we were having a lot of fun. I just lost track of the time."

"Listen, young lady!" said her mother. "That's no excuse! As for what time your friends' curfews are, it doesn't matter. I'm not their mother. I'm *your* mother! You are fifteen years old, Sarah! You want a later curfew? Well, coming home late is not the way to prove that you're mature enough for one. You are grounded for two weeks."

"Two weeks!" exclaimed Sarah.

"Sarah, keep your voice down," replied her mother. "Your father's sleeping. Even though tomorrow's Sunday, your father has to show some properties. He has to get up early. I don't want you waking him!"

"But, Mom!" exclaimed Sarah. "That's not—"

"Sarah," her mom interrupted, "if you say one more word, I'll make it three weeks. Now, we have to get up early for church tomorrow. I suggest you get to bed."

The Next Morning

"Sarah, it's eight o'clock!" her mother said, knocking on Sarah's bedroom door. "It's time to get up for church."

"I'm not going!" exclaimed Sarah through the bedroom door.

"Sarah!" her mother cried. "I am not having this argument with you! You need to get up now! I don't want to be late. It'll be hard enough to find a place to park! I'm losing my patience! Now get up!"

Sarah opened the door and glared at her angry mom. "I hate you!" she cried. She then slammed the door shut.

Before Sarah had slammed the door, she saw the look of devastation in her mother's eyes. She was expecting her mother to angrily knock on the door. But she didn't. A few minutes later, Sarah could hear her leave. Her mother's feelings must have really been hurt.

Good! thought Sarah. With that, she went back to bed.

A few hours later, her father came home.

"Sarah!" her father yelled.

Oh, just great! she thought. *Mom must have told him what happened. Now I'm really going to get it.*

Sarah opened her bedroom door and walked out into the hallway. She knew her father was going to be angry with her. But when she saw him, he wasn't angry. He was crying.

"Daddy, what's wrong?" asked Sarah.

Her father grabbed her and held her tight.

"Oh, sweetheart!" cried Robert. "I have something horrible to tell you. I just got a call from the state police. When your mom went to church this morning, she parked in the lot across the street. While she was in the middle of the crosswalk, a drunk driver ran a red light and hit her."

Sarah began to tremble in her father's arms as she looked into his eyes.

"Is she going to be okay?" Sarah asked as tears started welling up in her eyes.

"No, princess," her father cried. "She's gone."

***

Present Day

Sarah began to cry, and she looked at Todd.

"I don't think either one of us stopped crying for two days," Sarah said. "And it's all my fault. Our fight made her late. That's probably why she had to park across the street. Not only that, but my last words to her were that I hated her. I don't hate her. I love her. I miss her. If only I'd gone to church with her or even made my curfew, she'd still be alive today."

Todd put his arms around her and held her in a supportive embrace.

"Listen, Sarah," he began. "Life just happens sometimes. Your mother's death wasn't your fault. It was the fault of the rat bastard who not only decided to get drunk on a Sunday morning but was also stupid enough to get behind the wheel of a car."

"I understand what you are saying, but what if—" Sarah began, but Todd interrupted her.

"Look, Sarah, you can't play the what-if game all your life. It won't change the outcome. And if you keep looking back on how the past could have been different, you'll never move forward. Like the late, great John Lennon once said, 'Life is what happens when you're too busy making other plans,' and look what happened to him. You do know who John Lennon was, right?"

Sarah looked at Todd and smiled.

"Of course I do. He was in the Monkees."

Todd gave her an odd look and then realized she was kidding. They both burst out laughing. Then all of a sudden, they stared into each other's eyes. Without thinking, Todd leaned in and gave her a kiss. He realized what he was doing and quickly backed away.

Sarah was stunned. It was her first kiss. It was better than she had ever imagined. She looked up at Todd. His eyes were as big as saucers.

"I'm sorry, Sarah. I shouldn't have done that," he said. "For a second, I forgot you were a sixteen-year-old girl."

"It's okay," she replied. "I wasn't exactly fighting you off of me." She felt a chill in the air as a cold breeze began to blow. The entire situation was so eerie it frightened her.

"She is mine!" a hauntingly masculine voice declared.

Sarah looked at Todd. He all of a sudden had trouble breathing, and his eyes rolled back into his head. To her horror, he fell to the ground and began to convulse and seize. Blood poured out of his eyes, his nose, and his mouth.

"Todd!" she screamed. "Todd! Oh God, help him! Please! Someone call 911! Help!"

***

Jonathan had been driving around town, looking for Sarah. Wherever she was, he just couldn't find her. Had Michael found a way to take her already? Surely, Michael would have informed him if he had.

He had to find her before someone got hurt. He decided to check his voice mail. Perhaps either Sarah or Robert had called and left a message. There was one message. Jonathan listened to it. He was terrified by what it said.

"Hey, Jonathan, it's Robert," the message said. "I called Sarah an hour ago. She's fine. Now don't get upset, but she ran into Todd. He just took her out for a burger, and then he's bringing her right home. It's all completely innocent. My meeting with the developer just wrapped up, so I should be back soon. Anyway, I know you were concerned about her. I just wanted to let you know everything was okay."

Jonathan began to panic.

Dear God! No! thought Jonathan. *Please say Michael doesn't know!*
Just then, he heard Michael's angry voice inside his head.

"I warned you, Jonathan! But you didn't listen! You were supposed to keep an eye on her! Because of you, someone you care about is dead! He couldn't keep his damn hands—or his mouth—off of her! His soul now belongs to me!"

In a knee-jerk reaction, Jonathan slammed on the brakes.

"Oh my God!" cried Jonathan, "*Todd*!"

***

Chapter 6
At Last We Finally Meet

Lieutenant Eric Johnson was head of the local police department. Since it was a nice day, he decided to take his lunch break in the city park. He and his wife had moved to the sleepy little seaside town after their youngest daughter, Erica, started college.

He had worked for the NYPD for twenty years and thought the town would be an ideal place to spend his remaining years with the police force—until he started getting inundated with calls about possible supernatural occurrences, mainly having to do with the legendary manor.

Most of those calls were from young women. They would actually call and report that the manor itself was observing them whenever they would go near it. Lieutenant Johnson just passed it off as narcissism, paranoia, or both. Still, the old place was creepy. Most people in town tried to avoid going near it as much as possible.

I gotta get out of this nutty town, he thought as he was finishing his lunch. All of a sudden, he heard a young woman screaming.

"*Todd*!" she screamed. "*Todd*! Oh God, help him! Please! Someone call 911! Help!"

He looked up and saw her. She looked to be about the same age as his youngest daughter, Erica. He quickly ran over to see what was happening. When he got to the girl, he looked in horror at the young man lying dead in front of him. He then got down on the ground to check the young man's pulse.

"This is Lieutenant Johnson," he said on his police radio. "I need a bus sent to the city park on Main Street. No, this one is DOA."

The young woman looked up at the lieutenant.

"No!" she cried. "Todd? He can't be!" She threw her arms around him and held on tight.

Although it seemed unprofessional, he returned her embrace. He was a father and felt compassion for the crying girl.

"I'm sorry, sweetheart," he said solemnly. "There's nothing we can do. He's gone. What's your name?"

"S-Sarah, Sarah Gilmore," she replied.

"Gilmore?" he asked. "Are you related to the mayor?"

"He's my uncle," she told him. "And that's Todd, his brother-in-law."

Much to Eric's chagrin, a crowd was forming around them. He looked at Sarah Gilmore and began to worry. Her body was trembling, and she was breathing heavily.

"Listen, Sarah … listen, sweetie," he told her in a calming voice. "You need to breathe … slowly. You are starting to hyperventilate. Calm down. You don't want to go into shock. Why don't we go sit down, and we won't look at this anymore? You need to relax and calm down. Is there anyone you want me to call?"

Sarah looked at him with tears in her eyes and nodded.

"Yes, my dad," she replied.

"Do you have the number?" he asked.

'It's in the contact information on my phone,' she told him.

Eric found the number and proceeded to call Robert.

"Sarah!" he heard a man's voice cry.

As Eric looked over, he saw Jonathan running toward them.

Sarah ran over to her uncle and threw her arms around him.

"Oh, Uncle Jon!" she cried. "I don't know what happened. We were laughing and having a good time. Then, all of a sudden … I don't know. It was horrible. I've never watched a person die before."

"Mayor Gilmore, I'm sorry about your wife's brother," said Eric.

"Damn!" said Jonathan. "Why did this have to happen?"

"You know why!" a middle-aged woman yelled from the crowd.

Sarah turned around and saw the crazy hippie lady from the restaurant.

"It was her!" the woman cried, pointing at Sarah. "The manor killed him because it wants her! And it will kill till it gets her. I know. I'm a medium and an empath. I can sense both benevolent and malevolent spirts. I wouldn't get too close to her, Lieutenant. It may mistake your kind gestures as an attraction for her. Then you will suffer the same fate as the young man lying before us. I'm warning every man to stay away from her, for she is now the angel of death!"

"I'm not in the mood for any ghost nonsense today!" Eric snapped. "A young man is dead, and a young girl is terrified! I don't need anyone instigating a riot!"

Eric then looked at the body laid out before him. He had never seen anything like it. The poor young man had to be in either his late twenties or early thirties. There was a great amount of drying blood around every orifice of the young man's face.

This can't be natural causes, he thought.

"Sarah, what did you do before you guys walked in the park?" Eric asked.

"We ate lunch at that burger place over there, across the street," she replied as she pointed at it.

"Okay, I'll question the employees," said Eric.

"You don't think this was a murder, do you?" asked Jonathan.

"I don't know what to think," replied the lieutenant. "All I know is that the manner in which this young man died needs to be fully investigated. I've never seen anyone bleed like this from natural causes. By the way, Mayor Gilmore, how did you know to come here?"

"I didn't," replied Jonathan. "I-I just happened to be walking by and saw you with Sarah. I also noticed Todd's body lying on the ground."

The lieutenant suspected he was lying, but he didn't have any proof. He couldn't explain why he felt that way. Maybe it was just something in his gut. Or maybe it was because Mayor Gilmore was currently under investigation.

"Sarah, if you remember anything else or if you need help, here's my card," Eric told her. "I want you to call me, especially if you think you're in danger."

"Thank you," she replied. She looked at him with a sorrowful smile. Tears were still building up in her eyes. Backup soon arrived, and the lieutenant needed to start an investigation. Eric couldn't shake the feeling that she might be in some kind of danger. But he left Sarah with her uncle and headed for the burger place to start his investigation.

***

"I'm going to take you home, Sarah," said Jonathan. "I think it would be better for everyone if I took you where you belong."

"But Lieutenant Johnson called Daddy and told him to meet me here," she replied.

"Don't worry. I'll let your father know that you are going to be where you belong," he told her.

"Okay, Uncle Jon," Sarah replied.

"Sarah, Jonathan!" a voice cried.

Jonathan turned around and saw Robert running toward them.

Damn! thought Jonathan. *I almost had her.*

Sarah began to cry. She ran to her father and threw her arms around him.

"Daddy!" she cried. "Daddy, it was awful. Todd and I were having a nice time, and then all of a sudden, he just died the most horrible death. It was awful, Daddy. That nice policeman, the one that called you, heard me scream for help. He stayed with me until Uncle Jon showed up. Uncle Jon was about to take me home."

"Well, I'm here now," said Robert. "I can take her home."

"Sarah, did Todd by any chance try and kiss you?" asked Jonathan.

"Geez, Jonathan!" yelled Robert. "The poor man is dead. Give him a break!"

"I just meant ... Oh, never mind," said Jonathan.

Robert looked at him, as if trying to figure out what was going on with him.

***

Robert and Sarah then walked toward Robert's car.

"Daddy," Sarah began, "there was something else."

"What was it, princess?" asked Robert. "You know you can tell me anything."

"Daddy, I thought I heard … Oh, never mind," she said. "It's just my mind playing tricks on me."

"Well, if you decide it wasn't just all in your head," he told her, "please feel free to come talk to me."

He put his arm around her, and she leaned her head on his shoulder. They then got into the car, and Robert drove toward Jonathan's. All of a sudden, Sarah felt tired. She quickly dozed off in the car.

That's when she experienced a strange occurrence. Sarah had woken up, but she wasn't in her father's car. She was awake inside her own unconscious mind. She looked around and saw nothing but darkness. She was terrified.

"Where am I?" she called out. "Why am I here?"

"Because I brought you here!" the husky male voice answered. A dark figure appeared and slowly began to walk toward her. Her terror increased. The closer he got to her, the clearer his image became. She looked up at him, afraid of the man approaching her. She was scared that an evil-looking demon was coming toward her. To her surprise, however, he was probably the most beautiful man she had ever seen. Even so, she was still afraid to be in his presence.

"Who-who are you?" she asked. Her body began to tremble with fear.

He gazed upon her with a loving smile and then gently rubbed the back of his fingers down her cheek.

"Don't be afraid, Sarah. You already know who I am," he told her. "I am Michael, Michael Winworth, your fiancé."

***

CHAPTER 7
May I Have This Dance?

Sarah stared at him in fear, not liking the fact that he had touched her face. She found it creepy that this older man, a complete stranger, would touch her like that. Yet she could also not deny how handsome he was, standing there in all his nineteenth-century regalia, a true old-fashioned gentleman.

He was a tall man, a few inches taller than she was. He had a strong, chiseled jawline and a distinct Roman nose. His perfectly groomed facial hair gave him a most distinguished look. His full head of thick raven-black hair only accentuated his beautiful enigmatic ice-blue eyes.

Sarah was almost speechless, not knowing what to do or how to react to the situation.

He smiled at her and then bent to kiss her hand.

"Forgive me, my dear Sarah. It is impolite of me to stare at you," he said. "I have always prided myself on being a gentleman, and a gentleman never stares at a lady. However, a beggar can look upon a queen."

Suddenly, a full-length mirror appeared before her. To her surprise, she was now wearing a red ball gown, ruby tiara, and diamond necklace with a ruby pendant.

She looked back at him, still feeling nervous because of his constant amorous stare. She began to blush and was almost too embarrassed to look directly at him. Even though he knew what effect he was having on her, he extended his hand.

"May I have this dance, my lady?" he asked.

Not knowing what else to do, even though she felt uneasy because of him, she took his hand. He gently placed his other hand on her back.

Although she had no idea what was about to happen, she instinctively rested her other hand on his shoulder.

"Don't worry. I'll lead," he told her, and with that, he started to spin around with her. Then, all of a sudden, they were in a grand ballroom, and an orchestra began to play. It was the same ballroom she had seen when she had stared into the manor the first time.

As they moved along the dance floor, they kept staring into each other's eyes. She was still frightened but also mesmerized by him. *Those eyes!* They were beautiful yet strong. It was almost as if his eyes were not quite human. They stared into her very soul. She could easily get lost in them, while not even wanting to escape their powerful gaze.

"How are you doing all of this?" she asked. "I don't even know what dance we're doing. How am I able to do it?"

He let out a playful laugh.

"You're asleep, remember?" he told her. "I have taken over your unconscious mind by entering it. The dance we are doing is a waltz. You are more or less just moving along to the music with me."

"You've entered my mind?" she asked. She couldn't help but feel a little violated.

"Yes," he replied. "This is how I know so much about you. I know your favorite color is red—that's why I chose this ball gown for you. And as my queen, you deserve a matching tiara and the finest jewelry. I am also showing you what the grand ballroom of the manor once looked like. But most important, I wanted to show you what I look like. I hope my appearance is quite pleasing to you."

"Y-yes, you are very handsome," she said. Although she did find him handsome, she was still nervous about the entire situation. Sarah began to tremble in his arms.

"I'm glad you think so, my dear, because I find you extremely beautiful," he said with longing in his eyes.

He could tell she was nervous by how evasive she was trying to be. Michael found this both charming and amusing.

"Th-thank you," she replied. "Is that Mozart?" She was trying to change the subject. She could see and feel his lust for her. It was frightening for her, seeing him stare at her like he was a hungry wolf and she his meek, helpless, and timid prey. No other man, that she knew of anyway, had ever looked at her like this.

"Yes, it is," he said and smiled at her. "I knew you were a smart girl. Are you enjoying our engagement party? You will make a perfect bride."

She looked at him, feeling a combination of fear and confusion. She was about to say something, but he stopped her. He let go of her hand and placed his index finger on her lips.

"Shhh," he told her, "I know what you are about to say, but this is not the time for negativity. This is a celebration, just for you, my love. I don't want anything to spoil this precious moment." With that, he took her hand again, and the music became louder.

The longer they danced, the more hypnotic the music became. It was almost as if she were becoming intoxicated. She closed her eyes and let the music take over her mind. She began to fall under his spell and let out a contented sigh.

"I love you, Sarah," he whispered in her ear. His hot breath on her neck made her entire body quiver with desire. Goose bumps formed up and down her entire body. She was as untouched as a field of pure white newly fallen snow. But even she knew the feeling of arousal that he was causing in her.

She opened her eyes and stared deeply into his. He then leaned in and gave her a passionate kiss. Still under his spell, she didn't even try to stop him. It was her first passionate kiss. It almost took her breath away, and she hungered for more. Sarah was more than eager to reciprocate his passion. As she did, it put her even deeper into a trance.

"Sarah," he whispered again in her ear, "soon, you and I will be together forever."

That phrase actually frightened her, so much so that it not only broke his hypnotic spell but suddenly woke her from the dream. She let out a startled gasp as she came out of her deep sleep.

The gasp surprised her father, who was still driving her back to Jonathan's. He could see the shocked look upon her face. She was wide-eyed and appeared confused.

"Are you okay, sweetheart?" Robert asked. He was so concerned about her, wondering how much Todd's death might be affecting her.

"I'm fine," she said. "I just had a weird dream."

"I guess," he replied. "You were talking in your sleep."

"What was I saying?" she asked out of curiosity.

"I don't know," he told her. "You were just mumbling."

"How long was I out?" she asked him.

"Um, I'd say almost two minutes," he told her.

"Really?" she asked. "The dream seemed a lot longer." She felt so confused about everything that had just happened.

"Well, I guess linear time only exists in the real world," he said. "Honey, are you okay? Do you want to talk about it?"

"I'm fine, Daddy," she replied.

She didn't know what to say. She didn't even know that he would believe her. All she knew was that she had been seduced by a dangerously alluring man, and that scared the hell out of her.

***

CHAPTER 8
Lost Innocence

After Sarah, Robert, and Jonathan arrived back at Jonathan's home. Sarah was still traumatized by the events of the day. First was witnessing Todd's gruesome and untimely death. Then there was meeting his murderer. It had to have been him. She recognized his voice, as well as the seductive spell that his ghostly apparition held over her.

Sarah hated herself for letting Michael affect her the way he did. She knew he was the one who had killed Todd, and she knew why. She may have been young and naive, but she wasn't stupid. Yet she let his handsome face and dangerous charm seduce her so easily.

The three of them sat down together for dinner. Robert looked at his daughter and then his brother. No one seemed to want to talk—or eat.

"Sarah, are you all right?" he asked.

"Not really, Daddy," she told him somberly. "I just can't get that horrible image out of my head."

"Do you want to talk about it, sweetheart?" her father asked.

"It was just so horrible," she answered. "Please don't be mad at me."

"For what, Sarah?" her father asked.

"Todd and I were just sharing a moment, and it got the best of us. I let him kiss me. But then he remembered how old I was, and he immediately pulled away from me, and then he apologized. Then I felt a cold chill. I thought I heard a man's voice, and then it happened."

"What man's voice?" asked Jonathan.

"I don't know," she responded. That was only a half truth. At the time, she didn't know. However, she knew now that it was Michael.

"Then he struggled to breathe," she continued. "Something strange

39

killed him. Then a creepy hippie lady told everyone in the park that it was my fault."

Sarah began to cry. Her father, who had been seated next to her at the dinner table, immediately leaned toward her. He wrapped his arms around her and pulled her into a loving embrace. She leaned her head against his shoulder and began sobbing profusely. A waterfall of tears came pouring out of her, as her father held her tight.

"It's not your fault, Sarah," her father told her.

Robert also had tears in his eyes. Her father then kissed the top of her head. She looked up at her father and smiled.

"I'm just not hungry," she said. "Would you mind if I skipped dinner? I just want to take a shower and go to bed."

"I don't mind, sweetheart," he replied. "Do you mind, Jonathan?"

"No, of course not," Jonathan responded. "You've had a rough day; we all have."

"Good night, Daddy. Good night, Uncle Jon," she said to them.

She then gave each of them a peck on the cheek before heading up to take a shower.

***

"Poor kid," said Robert, "Having to watch something as horrific as that, only to have some crazy lady screaming that it was her fault. That was the last thing she needed. I don't get this town. How could anyone think that Sarah was responsible for Todd's death?"

"You'd be surprised and why," Jonathan said and sighed. "Well, I now have the unpleasant task of trying to get through to Karen and Todd's parents. Not only have they lost their only daughter, but now they've lost their only son."

"I know that's going to be rough for you," said Robert. "Is there anything I can do?"

"Just know that I truly love both you and Sarah," replied Jonathan. "We'll always be brothers, no matter what. If there ever comes a time when you may get angry with me, just keep in mind that we're family. If you ever need me, Robert, I will always be there for you. I mean, even if I may be the last person you want to ever see. Just remember that I love you."

"Well, that's kind of an odd thing to say to me. Are you planning on doing something to make me angry? You know, if I didn't know any better, I would think you're planning on betraying me somehow," said Robert.

"No, of-of course not," replied Jonathan with a nervous laugh. "It's just that with both Karen and Todd dying so suddenly, I just realized how important siblings are."

"I feel the same way about you, Jon," said Robert. "Oh, and I guess I owe you an apology."

"For what?" asked Jonathan.

"Don't get me wrong," replied Robert. "I'm not mad at Todd for kissing Sarah. Things like that can happen. I'm not going to have anger toward someone who just died, but I guess you were right about him."

"Yep," sighed Jonathan. "I guess so."

***

Sarah had just showered and finished drying her hair. After leaving the bathroom, she headed to the guest room, where she had been staying. There was another cold chill.

"It's just the air conditioner," she kept telling herself. "You just got out of the shower; it's normal to be cold." She then removed her robe and let it slowly fall to the ground.

After it hit the floor, she had a creepy feeling that she wasn't alone. It was as though she was being watched. All of a sudden, the chill started to envelop her. It was if a blanket of cold air was wrapping around her body. Then she heard him.

"Relax, Sarah," Michael's husky voice whispered. *"As I said before, you are the love I've been searching for. You will soon be mine and only mine forever. Don't be frightened. I just need to sample my future bride. Your beautiful young body is too enticing to just look upon. Just know that what I'm doing is out of love. I'm going to show you pleasures you've never even imagined."*

Sarah became frightened and began to tremble as she felt his cold, invisible presence start to caress her naked flesh. She tried to scream for help, yet something was silencing her. The young virgin had barely even been kissed. Todd had been her first, and that was by accident.

She became terrified as she could feel his cold lips press against hers, and then he forced his tongue into her mouth. His hands gently teased her firm, supple breasts and slowly began moving down between her thighs. Yet there was no one there.

Michael's spirit kept her in place, and she was completely helpless. She was unable to move or cry out for help. He gently began to make his way down between her legs.

To her horror, she felt cold lips pressed against her Pandora's box as he gently slipped his tongue into her opening. The frightened girl let out a gasp as his tongue began exploring her untouched clit. Her body betrayed her, and she started to moan. She tried to fight the raw orgasmic pleasure that was coursing between her legs. But she couldn't, or at least didn't want to. Instead, she moaned even louder.

Michael began to laugh.

"One set of pretty pulsating lips wants to tell me no, while another set is begging me for more," his voice sneered.

Warm tears began to stream down her face.

"Please stop," she begged. "Where are you, Michael? What are you? Why did you kill Todd?"

Michael stopped, and she could feel him caressing her body. He wrapped his arms around her in a loving embrace.

"Please don't cry, my angel," Michael pleaded. *"I will never hurt you, I promise. Just let me love you, and I will grant your heart's every desire. Soon, you will be my bride, and you will please me as I will please you. I'm sorry about Todd, but he kissed you, he tried to take what's mine. No one takes what belongs to me. You, my dear, my future bride, belong to me."*

"Never!" she cried. "I will never marry you or let you control me."

"But you don't understand, my love," he explained. *"I can possess anyone I want, whenever I want. Everyone and everything in this town belongs to me! That includes you and your father. If you don't willingly marry me, your father will have to die just as Todd did. You have already seen what I can do. I can instantly stop anyone's heart. Once I do that, their soul is mine and serves me. I do need another butler, and your father seems perfect for the job."*

"No, please don't hurt him," she cried. "My mother died six months ago! He's all I have left. He's my family."

"No, my angel," Michael told her. *"From now on, I will be your family. Don't be frightened. Once I take you as my living bride, I can restore the manor. It will be a permanent void between life and death. I will become*

corporeal again, and we will be together for all eternity. I need your life-force to sustain the void."

Sarah became frightened by what he had just said.

"W-what do you mean, my-my life-force?" she asked in fear.

"Don't worry, my love," he said reassuringly. *"It will not harm you. Originally, I was going to be the life-force, but the original object of my desire stabbed me in the back, literally. I need to marry a living being to restore the void, as well as the manor. I could have used any woman, but I wanted to wait for the perfect one. I waited two centuries to find one such as you, and now that I have, I will never let you go."*

"Why me?" she cried.

"Because I love you," he said.

"How?" she asked. "You don't even know me."

"Oh, but I do, my love," replied Michael. *"I was enchanted not only by your outer beauty but by your inner beauty as well. Your inner beauty makes your outer beauty shine tenfold. I can enter the mind of anyone who comes within a certain perimeter of the manor. I experienced your whole life, from conception up until our first encounter."*

"Th-that's impossible," she cried.

Michael began to laugh.

"Believe me, my dear," he began. *"You have no idea how powerful I really am. When you first stared with wonder into the manor. You stared into its soul, or rather my soul. I have been in the minds of many women before you. But I never fell in love with anyone, not until I met you. It is too late. You have enchanted me."*

"Please, please stop raping me," she pleaded.

"I would never do that to you, Sarah," he told her. *"I love you. Making love is not rape."*

"Holding me in place, keeping me from screaming for help, and molesting me without my consent is rape," she argued.

Michael began to sigh.

"You're right. I'm sorry, my dear," Michael replied. *"I just lost control of my own urges. Forgive me, but you also have to remember that I come from a less-enlightened time. But it's more than that. I've waited for you for two hundred years. I wasn't thinking. You, my angel, are the only person I would*

never want to hurt. I promise, Sarah, I will never hurt you. And I would violently destroy anyone who would."

"I don't believe you," cried Sarah.

Once again, Michael began to sigh.

"Perhaps it's this setting," said Michael. *"I think you and I need someplace more … romantic."*

She didn't like the sound of that.

"Wh-what do you mean?" she asked.

"Listen to my voice, Sarah," he told her. *"Get into bed. I will make you fall asleep again, just like I did this afternoon. I am going to enter your mind, your unconscious mind, just as I did earlier."*

"What are you going to do to me?" she asked in fear and uncertainty.

"Don't be afraid. I am going to be loving and gentle," he said reassuringly. *"I am going to take your beautiful young body, and you will feel pleasures you didn't even know were possible."*

She could feel him taking control of her mind. She tried to fight him, but it was to no avail. He was too powerful and too strong willed. She did everything he told her to do, before she even realized what was happening. As she lay in bed, she became frightened, worried about what he might be planning to do to her.

"Please don't—" she began, but he stopped her.

"Don't worry," he began. *"I am going to use your unconscious mind again and take you someplace special, someplace almost as beautiful as you, and we are going to make passionate love together. Don't worry, my sweet. I promise you'll enjoy it. After all, a woman's first time should be special."*

***

CHAPTER 9
To Sleep Perchance to Dream

Sarah could feel herself being pulled into sleep. Once again, she was fully aware of her current plane of existence. She was in her own unconscious mind, again surrounded by darkness. The darkness soon began to fade. She heard the ocean, felt its warm breeze, and smelled the fresh sea air.

As the darkness completely faded away, it was replaced by a beautiful sunset over the ocean.

The entire area around her was enchanting, and she had never seen anything like it. She enjoyed taking in the scene that was unfolding in front of her. The now bright-red sun reflected upon the water in a crimson explosion. She was entranced by the vision surrounding her until she remembered why she was there.

Sarah knew he was there, right behind her. She could feel his rock-hard chest, and torso pressed against her back. His muscular arms came from behind and wrapped around her, pulling her into his firm embrace. She was frightened as he kissed the top of her head. He breathed in the scent from her hair.

"You smell divine," he whispered. "What do you think of this place? Do you like it?"

"It's beautiful," she replied. "Where are we?"

"The Amalfi Coast, Italy, around 1816," he told her.

After staring out at the ocean, she closed her eyes. She became frightened, knowing what was about to happen. Yet at the same time, she was intrigued. Still feeling uncertain, she opened her eyes. Although feeling nervous, she then turned around to look at him.

It was at that point that she saw what he was wearing. He was in a pair of nineteenth-century undergarments. She had to admit to herself that he was built rather well. She had never before seen a man with such a broad chest and shoulders. She then looked down and saw that she was in a short white negligee.

Michael cupped his right hand under her chin, gently lifted her head, and looked her straight in the eyes. He looked at her with a loving smile. She couldn't help but tremble, not only because she was afraid but because of his eyes. They were both powerful and beautiful, and they were extremely hypnotic.

"Please don't," she begged as she felt warm tears streaming down her face.

Michael gently wiped away her tears. He smiled, and he intensely stared into her eyes.

"Please don't what? Sarah," he asked in a soothing whisper.

"Please don't hurt me," she answered softly.

Tears continued to well up in her eyes. She knew why he had brought her there, and she knew he wasn't going to take no for an answer.

"No, Sarah," he whispered. "I would never hurt you. I love you. I just need you to relax. Everything's going to be all right, I promise. Don't be afraid, my dear. Give in to your desires, Sarah. Give in to me."

With a look of burning desire, he stared even deeper into her eyes. As he did so, she was losing the will to fight him. He smashed his lips into her's, devouring her as they were locked in a passionate kiss.

Michael now had total control of her body, as he slowly released her from the kiss. He smirked, and placed his hands on her shoulders. Slowly and gently, he moved the straps down her arms until her garment slowly fell to the ground. All the while, he kept his eyes locked onto hers. He then took a step back to gaze upon her.

"Beautiful," he said. "You are truly a goddess."

She couldn't fight him physically or verbally, but she was scared of the lustful look upon his face. His eyes darkened, and a wicked smile appeared. Whatever he was doing to her, she could not stop him, nor did her body want to stop him.

He then gently scooped her up and carried her to a large blanket along the beach. With great care, he laid her down upon the blanket. After standing up, he kept looking at her with a lustful smile. She watched in fear as he slowly removed his only piece of clothing. Her face began to blush. It was the first time she had ever seen a man naked.

Michael slowly got down on his knees and began to straddle her. He then lay on top of her and stroked each cheek with the back of his fingers. He looked at her with love in his eyes.

"You are so beautiful, Sarah," he whispered. "I've never known any other woman like you."

Michael placed a passionate kiss upon her lips. As he did, his tongue slipped in between them. Her mind wanted him to stop, but it was as if her body wasn't listening.

"What are you doing to me?" she asked. She felt as though she was going into a trance. A feeling of euphoria took over her entire body, and she could feel herself becoming aroused.

"I'm going to make you feel good," he told her.

Michael then moved his mouth down to her neck. He began laying wet, openmouthed kisses upon her. The more he did, the less she wanted to fight.

"How are you doing this to me?" she asked.

"I am lowering your inhibitions," he whispered as he continued kissing her neck. "On some level, you want me more than you know. I have been inside your mind and explored all aspects of it. I know your deepest and darkest desires. I know more about them than you do. If you didn't want me on some level, you wouldn't let me continue. Do you want me to continue, Sarah?"

She then leaned her head back and closed her eyes.

"Yes," she whispered. She was surprised she had said that. Consciously, she wanted him to stop, but somehow, her body was now in control over her mind. The more he kissed her, the more her body craved him.

He slowly moved his lips down to her breastbone, leaving a trail of wet kisses along the way. While one hand gently caressed one of her soft, supple breasts, he placed his lips upon the other breast. His mouth pleasured her. She began to moan as his tongue and his lips sucked and teased her breast. He had the touch of an angel but the hunger of a demon.

At the same time, he was gently caressing the other breast, while delicately rubbing its nipple. The more he did this, the harder they became. Michael lifted his head to look at her and smiled. She knew her own facial expressions were letting him know that she was more than enjoying his passion.

He then pressed his lips against her neck, and he kissed his way down to the middle of her waist. All the while the touch from his lips and the delicate strokes of his fingers were leaving a trail of goose bumps upon her soft, naked flesh.

When he got to her panties, he gently ran his index finger down to her most sacred area. With a soft touch, he began to rub his finger along her opening slit. She let out another moan, and her body responded another way. She could feel her panties getting wet. They were getting wet for him, and she wanted him to do more.

It was then that he removed them. He pulled them ever so delicately down her legs. As he looked down, he gently spread her thighs apart. This caused her opening to reveal more of her most forbidden fruit, and he longed to taste her sweet nectar.

"So lovely and pink," he said and smiled. "Virgins always taste the sweetest. Do these pretty, pulsating lips taste as good as the ones around your mouth?" he asked.

Slowly, he began caressing her opening with his fingers. She couldn't help it and let out a pleased sigh. But the more he touched her, the more she began to moan. Obviously pleased by what he had just accomplished, he let out a slight chuckle.

"So young, so beautiful, so delicate," he began, "an innocent lost lamb in the clutches of the big bad wolf."

He sat up as a devious smile widened upon his face. He then began to run his fingers through her hair. She closed her eyes as he tucked a strand of her hair behind her ear. His touch was gentle yet provocative. He leaned down and whispered in her ear.

"Such fiery hair, above and below," he seductively whispered. "Some illustrations of Little Red Riding Hood give her red hair. Perhaps a perfect analogy, since I'm the big bad wolf. And you, my dear, my helpless but definitely not hapless prey. Do you know the fable?"

"Yes, of course," she replied, feeling confused. "Why-why would you even bring it up?"

Michael gently placed his index finger upon her forehead and ran it down her face all the way down to her breastbone. His delicate touch caused her to breathe heavily as her body began to writhe.

"I want you to quote what Little Red Riding Hood says to the wolf, when he's disguised as her grandmother," he whispered to her.

Sarah was afraid yet aroused at the thought of whatever he had in mind. She was scared of whatever he was planning on doing to her, and yet she craved more. Her mind didn't want her to feel this way, but her body had other ideas.

"W-what big ears you have!" she said.

He leaned his head down and began to whisper in her ear.

"The better to hear you scream in ecstasy, my dear," he responded.

"What, what big eyes you have," she said as her breathing became heavier. Her body began to melt as she felt his hot breath against her skin.

"The better to gaze upon you with hunger, my dear," he groaned. Then he too began to breathe heavily.

She turned her head to look at him. Sarah could see the lust that was burning in his eyes. She began to tremble in both fear and ecstasy.

"Wh-what sharp teeth you have!" cried Sarah.

His lips slowly crept into a wicked smile, and it widened upon his face.

"The better to eat you with, my dear!" Michael growled.

In an instant, he pushed her thighs apart. He hungrily began to feast upon her opening, as he aggressively devoured her virgin core. With that, the tip of his tongue made its way inside and found her sacred and forbidden fruit.

The more he licked and teased it, the more a burning and almost unbearable throbbing pleasure began to build up between her thighs. She could barely contain herself, and she began to writhe and moan.

"That's right, angel," he said. "Fill my mouth with your sweet ambrosia."

Her body eventually couldn't take it anymore. She arched her back and let out a loud, orgasmic scream. She had completely obliged him, as her sweet nectar was released into his mouth. Quickly, he sat up, and he had a wickedly satisfied smile on his face. Triumphantly, he wiped off his mouth.

"I never had a woman react that way before," he said. "I don't know which was better, your loud orgasmic response or just how delicious your succulent juices really taste.

He then bent back down and smashed his mouth against hers. Both of them were breathing heavily. He had brought out a wild, sexual, animalistic part of her. She had never experienced such intense gratification before in her life. They looked into each other's eyes, and she then gave him a seductive smile.

"Tell me what you want, Sarah!" he demanded. "Don't hold back! I want you to tell me what you want me to do to you!" She was still breathing heavily, and her adrenaline was pumping. She looked up and stared into his eyes. Damn, those eyes!

"Say it, Sarah!" he demanded again.

Her animalistic desires were now in high gear. She felt an almost painful yet pleasurable throbbing heat between her thighs. Her entire body was now consumed with only raw, sexual aggression. It was unlike anything she had ever experienced. She looked at him, and she could feel burning desire in her eyes.

To her surprise, a phrase that would normally make her blush began rattling off of her own tongue.

"I want your hard throbbing cock inside of me." She uttered breathlessly.

Michael stared into her eyes. A devilish smile grew upon his lips.

"Such a bad little girl." He whispered.

With that, he aggressively grabbed her outer thighs and yanked her body toward him. He then rammed his member into her, letting out a triumphant yell. Michael kept thrusting harder, faster, and deeper into her. He was grunting his pleasure while she was moaning hers. Her hips began to thrust in rhythm with his. Simultaneously their bodies moved, engaged in a dance of raw unadulterated sexuality.

"We're both almost there, Sarah!" he screamed. "Scream for me again, my love! This time, I want it to be my name!" He kept thrusting and thrusting inside of her. Then, she could no longer handle the pressure buildup anymore. Again, she arched her back and let out her most passionate scream.

"*Michaelllll!*"

With a startled gasp, Sarah woke up from the dream. She looked around and saw that she was in her uncle's guest room. She got out of bed, turned on the light, and pulled back the covers. The sheets were soaking wet with sweat, and there was a more concentrated wet spot on the bottom sheet.

Afraid because of what had just happened, she made her way into the bathroom. Crying, she quickly hopped into the shower. She kept scrubbing her body, but she just couldn't get clean. While leaving the shower running, she sat down on the floor. She held her knees against her chest. With that, she burst into tears and couldn't stop crying.

Her mind was now back in control. Even though her body had reacted to him, he had still forced her. He manipulated her body's desires into taking over her mind. It was no different than if she had been drugged. She didn't want it. She had been raped.

***

Chapter 10
A Father's Love

Sarah had sat on the floor of the shower crying for a good half an hour. She didn't know what to do. Her father would be the one she would normally go to, but she was afraid he wouldn't believe her. How could he? Sarah then got up, turned off the shower, and began to dry herself with a towel. Just then, there was a knock on the door.

"Sarah, are you all right?" her father asked. "It's two o'clock in the morning. Why are you taking a shower?"

She wrapped the towel around her, opened the door, and stepped into the hallway.

"I'm sorry, Daddy," she said. "I had a nightmare, or rather a night terror. I woke up sweating, and I just felt gross. I also need to change the sheets."

"Night terror?" he asked. "You haven't even had a bad dream since you were eight."

"Um, it was about Todd," she said, knowing that her father wouldn't believe the truth.

"I'm sorry," he said sympathetically. "Look, it's too late to change the sheets. Why don't you sleep in my room, and I'll sleep on the couch?"

"Daddy?" asked Sarah. "Can you stay with me tonight?"

"Sarah, you're sixteen years old," he told her. "It's a little inappropriate."

"Please, Daddy," she said. "I'm scared."

"Sarah, is there something you're not telling me?" he asked.

"What's going on? It's after two in the morning?" asked Jonathan, interrupting.

He came out of his room half asleep and joined them.

"Sarah had a night terror," explained Robert. "Jonathan, can I have an extra blanket?"

"Yeah, sure, they're here in the linen closet," he told Robert. "What do you need that for?"

"Sarah's afraid," Robert began. "She doesn't want to be alone. I'll just sleep on the floor, next to the bed."

"No, Daddy," said Sarah, "I don't want you sleeping on the floor."

"End of discussion, Sarah," her father replied. "You're my daughter. For you, I'd sleep on a bed of nails if I had to."

Jonathan had made his way to the linen closet and came back with a blanket for his brother.

"Well, I don't know about you guys," said Jonathan, "but I've gotta get back to sleep. Good night, you two."

As Jonathan made his way back to his room, Sarah went with her father into his room. She got under the covers, while her father did his best to get comfortable on the floor. *At least it's carpeted.*

"Good night, Daddy," said Sarah. "I love you."

"I love you too, princess," he responded.

***

Later that morning, Robert made his way down to the kitchen. This time, Jonathan was up first and was the one making the coffee.

"Would you like some coffee?" asked Jonathan. "How did you sleep?"

"Let me put it this way; I'll take my coffee black," he replied. "No offense, but your floor doesn't make the most comfortable bed. Plus, she was tossing and turning in her sleep all night. I know she's hiding something from me."

"All teenage girls are secretive," said Jonathan.

"I know, but most of them don't witness a gruesome death," said Robert. "She keeps saying that she gets cold chills and then hears a man's voice. I don't know. I think with Helen's, Karen's, and Todd's deaths being so close together, it might be more than she can handle. She really needs family right now, maybe even a therapist."

This could be the opportunity that I've been waiting for, thought Jonathan.

"I have an idea," Jonathan began. "While you're meeting with the real estate developer, I'll take her to lunch. Maybe it would be easier to talk to an uncle than a father."

"Thanks, Jonathan," said Robert, "but I'm going to postpone my meeting until tomorrow. Sarah and I need some alone time after what happened yesterday. Besides, you have an entire city to run. I'm sure you have some work you need to get done."

Damn! thought Jonathan. *Oh well, I guess they should have at least one last day together before Michael takes her away for good.*

"Well, if that's what you want," said Jonathan. "I know you're her father, not me. I would just advise not leaving her alone today. I would say keep an eye on her, in case she gets scared again."

Jonathan was afraid of any consequences that Michael might inflict on anyone who came in contact with her. Jonathan had to heed Michael's warning. If something happened to her, because no one was protecting her, Michael's wrath would be almost biblical.

"Of course, you're absolutely right," said Robert. "It wouldn't feel right leaving her alone today."

"Well then, I'll be down at city hall," said Jonathan. "Call me if you need anything."

"I will Zsa Zsa," said Robert, laughing.

"Zsa Zsa?" said Jonathan. "You know I hate that nickname. How did that start anyway? I don't remember."

"Because I was only two when you were born," replied Robert, "I had trouble pronouncing Jonathan, so it came out Zsa Zsa. Then, pretty soon, everyone in the family started calling you that, and after a while, it began to stick."

"Yeah, thank God that eventually faded into obscurity," said Jonathan.

"Well, I just might bring it back," said Robert with a wicked grin.

"You better not!" laughed Jonathan. "I really missed you, Robert."

"I've missed you too, Jonathan," Robert replied.

Jonathan started to leave, but he felt guilty over the bargain he made with Michael. He didn't want to hurt his brother or his niece.

"Robert, there's something I need to … to," Jonathan stammered, "to get at the store. Can I pick up anything for you?"

For a split second, he came close to telling Robert everything, but he decided that Karen's and Todd's souls were more important. Jonathan loved his niece, but he loved his wife more.

How he missed Karen's laugh and her beautiful smile. No matter what the cost, he had to save Karen. He just hoped that one day, Robert would forgive him.

"No, thanks, I'm good," said Robert.

With that, Jonathan decided he needed to head to work. He did have things to do, and he felt better knowing that Robert would be with her all day. He still needed to meet with the college in the neighboring town. It was now going to be pointless, as he didn't need to find a bride for Michael anymore, but he had to go through his daily routines. He didn't want anyone to become suspicious.

He was still going to have a life to live, even when all of this was over eventually. His only hope was that Robert, Karen, and probably even Todd would someday forgive him. He hugged Robert goodbye and then went to work.

***

Robert got on the phone and called the real estate developer.

"Look," said Robert to the developer over the phone, "I know the meeting's today, but I'm in the middle of a family crisis right now. Are you sure it can only be today?"

"I'm sorry, Robert," the developer replied. "It has to be today. I have a full plate. If we don't meet today, then you're not going to have a property to build your resort. I'm assuming your investors are not going to be all that understanding if you don't."

"All right," Robert said and sighed, "but I have to bring my daughter along with me."

"That's going to be extremely inconvenient," the developer replied.

"I don't care if you think it's inconvenient. Right now, she comes first," Robert tried to explain. "Look, I'm making the effort to see you today. Please, can you just oblige me?"

"If you insist." The developer sighed. "I just hope she doesn't get in the way."

"Thank you," said an annoyed Robert. "We'll meet with you in a couple of hours."

"Damn," he said after hanging up the phone. "Little snot nose piece of—"

"Morning, Daddy," said Sarah as she entered the kitchen. "I hope sleeping on the floor didn't keep you awake most of the night."

"Oh, Sarah. I didn't hear you come in here," he said to her. "Um, yes, I slept fine. Actually, I was just about to wake you. I wanted to spend the day with you, but I was unable to postpone today's meeting. However, I don't think it would be a good idea if you were alone today. So even though it's going to be boring, I think you should come with me. Then you and I can spend the rest of the day together—whatever you want to do, even if it ends up costing a lot of money. I don't care, my treat."

"Daddy, I'm not a little girl," she said. "I would just be in your way. You could leave me alone for a few hours. I'll be fine. I promise I won't leave the house. Then we can spend the day together."

"Are you sure?" he asked. "I'm not one hundred percent sure you should be alone today. Yesterday was extremely traumatic. I just don't think you should be alone right now."

"I'll be fine, Daddy," she answered.

Robert looked at her and sighed. *Perhaps it would be for the best.*

"All right," he told her. "But you have my cellphone number. If you need me for anything—and I do mean anything—you give me a call. I don't care how ridiculous it may seem. I want you to call me. Promise?"

"I promise, Daddy," she replied with a smile.

"Oh, wait, Sarah," he began. "I have something for you." He then pulled a jewelry box from his briefcase.

"I know your birthday was last month," he said, "but I have something else for you. I saw it in a local jewelry store, here in town, and I wanted to give it to you."

Smiling at her, he handed her the box. As she opened it, a big smile appeared upon her face. Her eyes widened, and her face lit up with delight. Inside the box was a beautiful gold locket.

"Daddy! It's beautiful!" she cried.

"I liked it because of the angel's wing," he told her. "Sort of a reminder that your mother is always watching over us. It's also eighteen-carat gold. That's actually the best gold for fine jewelry. Twenty-four carat gold, which is pure gold, is too soft to make jewelry."

"How do you know that?" she asked and smiled inquisitively.

He just looked at her and smiled.

"I'm your father," he replied. "I know everything. Anyway, read the inscription on the back."

"Sarah, always in our hearts."

"It's beautiful!" cried Sarah. She then gave her father a hug.

"Wait! Open it," he told her.

When she opened it, she saw the left side had a picture of her dad while the right had a picture of her mother.

"That picture of your mother," he explained, "I always keep a copy in my wallet. It's always been my favorite. You know, every day, you become more and more beautiful. You look a lot like her, including that fire-red hair."

Sarah couldn't help but smile at her father's compliment.

"When was this picture of you taken, Daddy?" asked Sarah.

"That is the other picture I always carry in my wallet," he told her. "It is a picture of me holding you the day you were born. I went to a local photo place to have the pictures copied. I know you're cropped out of the picture, but the locket was too small for the entire picture to fit. I just wanted you to be able to always see that look on my face. That's the look of a father whose daughter brings him his greatest joy in life."

He smiled at Sarah, and she smiled back. Both of them were starting to get a little teary eyed.

"Well," he continued, "the jeweler inscribed the back. Then he placed the individual pictures of your mother and me inside the locket. It cost a lot to speed up the process. It was worth it. If you really like it, promise me you'll always wear it. Please, I want you to never forget how much I love you. If you ever were to forget, for some strange reason, this locket will always be a reminder of my love for you."

"Daddy, I don't need a locket for that," she responded.

"I know," he told her, "but it's always nice to have a tangible reminder."

Tears began to well up in her eyes. She hugged him tight and gave him a peck on the cheek. She and her father then shared a loving gaze.

"I'll never take it off!" she cried. "I'll always wear it close to my heart. I love you, Daddy."

"I love you too, Sarah," he told her, wiping the tears from his eyes.

"Well, I need to compose myself before the meeting. I gotta go, sweetheart. Again, call me if you need anything. I mean that." He pointed at her.

"I will, Daddy," she replied with a smile.

He then left to meet with the developer. She was a little nervous about being alone. What if Michael tried to abduct her while she was all alone? There was no one there to protect her. But then again, how could he take her? He was a spirit. How would it even be possible?

The whole situation frightened her, as it was completely mind boggling. She needed a distraction. So she decided to sit down, relax, and watch TV. She kept looking at the locket and smiling. It gave her some feeling of comfort.

A half an hour later, the doorbell rang. Sarah looked out the window. To her surprise, it was the crazy psychic lady from yesterday, the same one who told everyone in the park that she, Sarah, was responsible for Todd's death. Sarah reluctantly opened the door.

"I'm glad you answered the door," the lady told her. "I was afraid you wouldn't—not that I would blame you. I was horrible to you yesterday. I want to apologize, but there was a reason I was acting so irrationally. As I said yesterday, I am both a medium and an empath. Normally, I can handle being around even malevolent spirits. But the one I sensed was angry, and it affected me in a negative way. I'm not just here to apologize. I'm here because I know you have questions."

"I only have two questions for you," Sarah replied. "Why should I believe you now? How do I know you're not here to hurt me?"

"Please, Sarah," the lady begged. "You need my help."

"I don't need anything from you!" cried Sarah. "Please just do us both a favor and go away."

"Sarah," said the lady, "your mother's spirit contacted me last night. She wants me to help you."

Sarah was now getting extremely upset. How dare this women bring up her mother!

"You're insane!" cried Sarah. "I don't believe you! First you tell an entire town that I was responsible for Todd's death. Now you're bringing up my mother? How did you even know that she died? What, are you stalking me? What kind of sick mind game are you playing? Lieutenant Johnson gave me his card! If you don't leave now, I'm going to call him!"

Sarah started to shut the door, but the woman placed her foot in the doorway, keeping Sarah from shutting it.

"Sarah," she said, "I know that Michael's spirit raped you last night."

Tears welled in Sarah's now widened eyes as she looked at the woman in total disbelief.

"How-how could you possibly know that?" Sarah cried.

"Helen, your mother, told me," the lady responded. "She's around you, watching you, always trying to protect you and your father. She wants me to warn you that you're in danger. May I come in? We need to talk. You are in a lot of danger, Sarah."

***

Chapter 11
A Mother's Love

Sarah was hesitant to let her inside. But because she feared Michael, Sarah decided to give the woman the benefit of the doubt.

"Come on in," said Sarah. "I'm sorry, what's your name by the way?"

"My name is Evangeline, Evangeline Nelson," she told her. "Your mother's spirit asked me to help you. I can communicate not only with spirits who have moved on but also those who refuse to leave earth's realm."

"Are you saying my mother hasn't moved on?" asked Sarah.

"No," said Evangeline. "Why would you assume that?"

"You just said she was with me," said Sarah. "Wouldn't that mean she's in earth's realm?"

"It's kind of hard to explain," Evangeline told her. "I'll do my best. I've asked how the afterlife works, but they tell me I can't comprehend it. It would be like trying to explain physics and string theory to an amoeba. Basically, God and the universe are all one and the same—different existences coinciding on different planes, and yet they all intersect. Just walking through a room, you can pass through millions of spirits existing in different planes of existence."

"Where do people end up, once they become spirit?" asked Sarah.

"Some in heaven, some in purgatory, and sadly, others in hell. Don't worry; your mother's in heaven."

Sarah felt relief upon hearing that.

"But then there are those who stay on earth's plane of existence," Evangeline continued. "They refuse to leave. It's hard, but they do find ways to avoid crossing over. These spirits refuse to let go of earthly experiences, and they refuse to move on."

"You mean like Michael Winworth?" Sarah asked.

"No," replied Evangeline. "He is another story. He was a dark witch. He tried to corrupt magic to create his own separate plane of existence, one where he himself would be, on some weird narcissistic level, God."

"How?" asked Sarah.

"You see, there are three types of witches," Evangeline began to explain. "Dark witches twist and corrupt magic for their manipulative purposes. Light witches tap into magic's purest form. Some witches can tap both sources. They are the most powerful and the most evil. They are the more shadowy of the dark witches. Those were the kind of witches that Michael Winworth and his mother were."

"I'm scared," said Sarah. "I don't know what to do. I don't want to go with him, but I know he's coming for me. If I don't marry him, he'll kill my father. My father will die like Todd and Aunt Karen."

"Sarah," began Evangeline, "I'm going to do something I rarely do. I can't guarantee how long it will last. It can abruptly end at any moment. I can channel your mother. She has the answers you are looking for—both about the situation going on here and the unfinished business between the two of you."

***

The meeting Robert had with the developer was all but a major bust. He couldn't keep his mind off of his daughter, and the developer could tell he just wasn't into it. He was actually able to reschedule, but everything seemed to be against him. Then, all of a sudden, the car just died on the way back to Jonathan's.

"Son of bitch!" he yelled. "Why isn't anything going right?"

He knew nothing about cars, so popping the hood would do him no good. It was times like this he wished he had taken auto shop instead of ceramics in high school. But he wanted to meet girls, not that he ever got a date out of the class. Well, he always had the automobile club. Unfortunately, with everything that had transpired last night, he forgot to charge the phone's battery.

"Can this day get any worse?" he asked. "Please, nobody answer that." Just then, it began to rain.

"Great, I had to go and open my big mouth." He sighed.

At that moment, out of sheer luck, a patrol car drove up.

"Can I help you, sir?" the officer asked.

"Please, my car broke down," he told him. "I have no idea about cars, and my cell battery is dead. So I can't call the automobile club for a tow. Also, I have to get home to my daughter. She really needs me right now."

"Hop in. I'll give you a lift. I can take you to the closest service station," he told Robert. "Normally, you'd have to sit in the cage in the back. But you're having a bad day, so I'll make an exception."

"That's awfully kind of you, Officer," Robert told him, getting into the car.

"By the way, it's lieutenant," he said to Robert. "Lieutenant Eric Johnson."

"I'm Robert, Robert Gilmore," said Robert. "Wait. Did you say Lieutenant Johnson?"

"Yep, I sure did," replied Eric.

"Oh!" exclaimed Robert. "We spoke on the phone yesterday. I'm Sarah Gilmore's father. I want to thank you for helping my daughter yesterday. She said you were very nice to her."

"You're welcome," said Eric. "I have three daughters of my own. I would just want someone to do the same for my daughters. My baby, Erica, is now eighteen. She just started her freshman year at NYU. Sarah reminds me of Erica a little. Some people just have that inner spark. Don't get me wrong. I have three lovely daughters. All kind, beautiful, and intelligent. But there's something inside of Erica. I just can't describe what it is. I just sense that it's there. Sarah has it too. One can always tell. How is Sarah, by the way?"

"She's okay, considering," Robert told him. "She had a night terror. I know she's more scared than she's letting on. I just can't get her to open up to me. That crazy woman from yesterday didn't help. Sarah's the type who feels guilty easily. I think she actually convinced Sarah that Todd's death was her fault."

"Yep," said Eric. "Sounds like my Erica. By the way, that crazy woman's name is Evangeline Nelson. She claims to be a medium. I would arrest her for committing fraud. She charges people for her services, but you can't arrest someone for being delusional. She really believes she has psychic abilities."

"You've got to be kidding me," said Robert.

"You think she sounds bad," said Eric. "You should hear about her son."

***

Evangeline and Sarah closed their eyes while holding each other's hands.

"Think about your mother, Sarah," said Evangeline. "Keep your eyes closed. If either one of us opens our eyes, it will break the link."

Sarah concentrated, but at the same time, she was skeptical. Normally, she didn't believe in psychics, but after the last couple of days, she thought anything was possible.

"Baby?" Sarah heard a voice say. It was in her mind, but it was her mother's voice. It was the exact same voice that had comforted her when she was a small child. She would recognize that voice anywhere. That same beautiful voice once sang her to sleep at night. Sarah began to cry.

"Mom!" Sarah exclaimed. "Is that really you?"

"I'm here, baby," said Helen's spirit.

"Mom, I'm sorry! I'm so sorry!" cried Sarah.

"For what?" asked Helen with love in her voice.

"It's my fault you died," said Sarah. "I'm also sorry that my last words to you were that I hated you. I don't, Mom. I love you, I miss you, and I need you now more than ever."

Tears kept flowing down her cheeks.

"Sarah, listen to me," Helen said soothingly. *"It was not your fault. Okay? Don't ever think that. Things happen. People always worry about what could have been done differently, but, baby, you can't. It was the fault of a man who shouldn't have been behind the wheel."*

"But, Mom!" cried Sarah. "What about the horrible thing I said to you? Not only that, but it was the last thing that I said to you. I'll never forget the sad look on your face!"

"Sarah," replied Helen. *"The sad look upon my face wasn't because of what you said to me that morning. It was there because the argument escalated to that point. You've been so traumatized by that one second of your life. You don't remember what I said to you. It was just as hurtful and just as brutal as what you said to me. I said it right before you told me you hated me. Think, Sarah. You have to remember what I said. As hard as it's going to be, it's the only way you'll see why it wasn't your fault. What did I say, Sarah?"*

Just then, Sarah remembered her mother's scathing words, and she burst into tears. It was hard, but she kept her eyes shut. She didn't want to break the link.

"Y-you said your life would have been a lot easier if I had never been born," Sarah cried. "I forgot."

"Sarah, do you hate me?" asked Helen.

"No," cried Sarah.

"Then you must realize that I never, at any time in my life, ever regretted giving birth to you," said Helen, *"You were little my angel. And maybe my life would have been a lot easier, but it wouldn't have been as much fun."*

"But I don't know if I can ever forgive myself," cried Sarah.

"Sarah, listen," replied Helen, *"You need to start forgiving yourself. We all say things we don't mean. Unfortunately, it's usually to the ones we love the most. Just know that I love you and your father. Also know that I am in a good place, and I am always watching the both of you. I am always around the two of you. You just can't see me. But, sweetheart, I'm there."*

"Mom," Sarah said, "Evangeline said you told her about last night."

"Yes, baby, I'm sorry he hurt you," Helen cried. *"I know you need motherly advice; that's why I'm here. Sweetheart, don't feel guilty. You didn't want it, and you didn't deserve it. He manipulated your mind and your body."*

"But I was attracted to him," said Sarah, "and I have had fantasies about … about being raped. Not only that, my body reacted to him. He said he couldn't make me give in unless I wanted him on some level. I mean, I can't even believe some of the disgusting things that I said. I was just too caught up in his passion."

"Sarah, listen to me," said Helen. *"There is nothing wrong with having those fantasies. There's nothing wrong with you for having them. It is a perfectly natural fantasy that most women have. Just because you fantasize about it, doesn't mean you want or deserve it."*

Sarah began to feel better about herself.

"Also just because you find a man attractive doesn't mean that it isn't rape if he forces you," Helen continued. *"Spirits that don't move on, they can't let go of the pleasures they get from life. They have sexual desires, but they are incapable of their own sexual gratification. They need a living human to experience it. He used your own body's sexual desires against you. Once he got you aroused, he began to feel your gratification as if it were his own."*

"How?" asked Sarah, both scared and confused.

"Your sexual energy gave him sexual energy," Helen explained. *"It was like a snowball effect. The more you gave him, the more he threw back at you. You began to fuel each other's sex drives. Every sexual pleasure you felt, he also felt. The only way a spirit can experience an orgasm is if their victim does. That's why you acted the way you did—not because you wanted him to, because he manipulated you. Sarah, do you understand now?"*

"Yes," Sarah cried, "I've waited so long, wanted so much, to talk to you about all of this. I thought I was some sort of deviant for ever having such fantasies. I even thought that I had set women back two hundred years. It's nice to know that I have no reason to feel ashamed."

"Listen, Sarah," Helen began. *"We don't have much time. I can't stay much longer. This man, Michael, is evil, but he is actually in love with you. However, he's a sociopath. That makes him extremely dangerous. He will stop at nothing until he has you. He will go through whomever you love to possess you. You and your father have to leave now! Sarah, whatever you do, as hard as this is going to be for you to accept, you can't trust—"*

Bang! A gun had fired on the lock of the front door. The perpetrator, holding a shotgun, then kicked the door open. The loud noise caused both Evangeline and Sarah to break the link.

"Oh my God!" cried Evangeline. "What the hell are you doing here?"

"Hello, Mother!" the man yelled. "Didn't you miss your little boy? Well, I hope so. Because I've been secretly following you around for the last couple of days. A couple buddies and I escaped prison recently. I thought maybe they would want to meet my bitch of a mother! That's her, fellas, the one who helped them send me up the river! The one who testified against me, *her only son! Her only child! She accused me of raping those girls!*"

With an evil smirk, he then turned his attention to Sarah. Afraid, Sarah began to back up as he came toward her. Before she could do anything, his friends grabbed her from behind. They held her in place, right in front of him. Sarah began to cry and tremble with fear. Her predator then gently grabbed her chin.

"Well, well, well," he began in a mock-soothing, creepy voice. "Look what we have here. Aren't you just the sweetest little thing? What's your name, princess?"

***

CHAPTER 12
The Lamb in the Lion's Den

"I asked you a question, princess. What's your name?" he asked.

Sarah stood there trembling. She could see the lust in his eyes. It was the same look that Michael had, but there was no love involved this time.

"Leave her alone, Alex," snarled Evangeline. "This has nothing to do with her."

Alex turned around to his mother, smiled, and then punched her right in the face. The blow was so hard his mother hit the floor. Sarah screamed and tried to go to Evangeline. However, Alex's cohorts were able to hold her back. Evangeline tried to get up, but Alex just kicked her square in the stomach.

"Did I say you could get up, bitch!" screamed Alex.

Both Sarah and Evangeline were now crying. Alex then turned his attention back to Sarah.

"I'm only going to ask you one more time, sweetheart," Alex said impatiently. "What's your name?"

"S-Sarah," she replied. Her body trembled in fear as she began to cry. Sarah felt both meek and helpless.

"Tell me, Sarah, do you attend the girls' college?" asked Alex.

"No," replied Sarah, "I'm only sixteen. I'm still in high school."

"Alex, don't do this!" cried his mother.

Alex looked back at his mother and kicked her in the face, which completely knocked her unconscious. Her nose and her mouth were now bleeding profusely. Sarah just cried, looking at her in horror. Alex then turned his attention back to Sarah.

"You know what, Sarah?" said Alex. "I hated high school. You know why? Because of rich little stuck-up cunts like you, who thought they were too good for me. Tell me, Sarah, do you think you're too good for me?"

"No," she said, trembling in fear.

Alex just looked at her and smiled. Then his demeanor suddenly changed, and he began gritting his teeth.

"Lying bitch!" he screamed, and he backhanded her across her left cheek.

"Hey, easy, Alex," said one of the goons sarcastically. "You don't want to damage that pretty face. Well, at least not until we're done with her. Besides, you're making her cry."

All three men began laughing at Sarah's fear.

"Is that right, princess?" asked Alex. "Am I making you cry? Because my friends and I can make you feel real good."

He was rubbing her face with the back of his knuckles. He made her feel sick to her stomach. In both fear and revulsion, she turned her head away while letting out a disgusted sigh. She realized she was about to be raped again, except this time, her attackers weren't going to manipulate her into liking it. She could feel someone grabbing some of her hair from behind.

"She smells delicious," said one of the attackers.

Alex kept looking at her. He then began to whisper in her ear, "Do we make you scared, Sarah? Do we, baby? I bet we do, and I bet it's just turning you on. Those little panties of yours must be soaking wet by now—just thinking of what we're going to do to that cute little body of yours."

Sarah closed her teary eyes. By now, the three of them had her completely surrounded. She wished her cellphone wasn't in her room. More than anything, she wanted to call the police.

"Please don't," she pleaded with tears in her eyes. "Please, besides my father should be home any minute."

Alex just kept staring at her with an evil grin slowly creeping up on his face.

"Is this your house, Sarah?" asked Alex. "Because I know it's not my mother's. She could never afford a place like this. See, I've been following her for two days now. I saw her little tantrum in town yesterday. Imagine my surprise when we saw you here. I would think you wouldn't want anything to do with that batshit crazy bitch. Is it true, Sarah? Does an entire mansion really want to fuck you?"

Sarah ignored the second question.

"This is my uncle's house," she told him. "He's the mayor, and my father will be home soon."

"Oh, this is the mayor's house," said Alex sarcastically. "I guess we'd better leave, right, boys?"

They laughed again, watching her cry.

"I'm not that worried if your daddy or your uncle, the mayor, comes home," said Alex. "See there's three of us, we have you, and I have a shotgun. I doubt Daddy will be much of a problem. You know what I remember about the rich little stuck-up bitches from high school? They were either prick-teasing prudes or slutty whores. Tell me, Sarah, which one are you?"

"None of your damn business," she replied.

"Oh, you've got quite the foul little mouth on you," said Alex. "I think I'll have to wash it out." He then smashed his lips to hers and forced his tongue between her lips. She kept moving her head, but it was no use. No matter how much she struggled, he was not going to stop until he was done. After finally stopping, he had completely repulsed her. She then spit in his face.

"*You bitch*!" he screamed. "Looks like I'm gonna have to teach you some fucking manners!" He then punched her in the stomach. The only reason she didn't fall to the floor was because of the two goons still holding on to her. Alex backhanded her face two more times, causing her upper lip to bleed.

Sarah couldn't stop crying. Alex then grabbed her blouse and ripped it open, exposing her chest in nothing but her bra. With a lustful smile, Alex began to lick his lips.

"Nice tits, princess!" he told her. "What a nice gold locket. Guess I'll get to have a souvenir of our time together. Don't worry, I'll wait till were done with you before I rip off it of that pretty little neck of yours."

"No!" cried Sarah. "Please! My father gave it to me. It's the most precious thing I own. I promised him that I would never take it off. It's a reminder of how much he loves me!" She pleaded with him, hoping that there was just the tiniest amount of human decency somewhere in his soul. She was sadly disappointed.

"You think I give a shit!" he exclaimed. "You stupid little whore. What did you have to do to get your daddy to give you that? Did you have to blow him? Well, wasn't that nice of your daddy. My daddy used to get drunk and used to beat the living shit out of me, my mom, and my little sister. Then he'd make me watch as he'd rape my little sister! You know what he gave her?"

Sarah didn't answer.

"*I asked you a question! Do you know what he gave her?*" screamed Alex. "*Answer me, bitch!*"

"N-no!" cried Sarah.

"He gave her a good bash with a crowbar, right upside the head!" exclaimed Alex, "He killed her! His only daughter! My only sister. You know why, princess?"

"No!" cried Sarah as she sobbed profusely.

"He told me to never trust anything that can bleed for five days and live!" replied Alex, "but I was too stupid to listen! I killed that motherfucker! I stabbed him right in the heart! But I killed the wrong parent."

Sarah closed her eyes. She didn't want to hear anymore. But she knew she didn't have a say in the matter. So she had no choice and reluctantly listened as he continued.

"Then my own bitch of mother, that stupid cunt who thinks she can talk with the dead," yelled Alex, "the same woman who had no problem testifying against me, when I was brought up on five charges of rape, she didn't protect me or my sister. My father was right! You're all a bunch of lying whores!"

Sarah was crying. She looked at him with a feeling of both fear and pity. She had never before heard such a tragic story.

"I-I'm sorry," she cried.

Alex began to laugh.

"You honestly think I want your pity, you stupid bitch!" exclaimed Alex as he harshly grabbed her jaw. "All I want from you is to spread your legs and then beg me for your worthless life!"

Alex then trailed his index finger from her chin down to her breastbone.

With a look of lustful desire upon his face, he stared her straight in the eyes. Then he leaned in and whispered in her ear, "Make 'em bounce."

Sarah was horrified by what he had just said. She had never heard anyone say anything more disgusting in her entire life. She couldn't believe that for a short time, she had actually felt sympathy for this man. More tears began to well up in her eyes, and she closed them tight. She didn't say a word, but she shook her head.

"Are you trying to tell me no, sweetheart?" he yelled.

Sarah opened her eyes and then looked straight at him, but she didn't respond.

"Well, guess what, princess?" he said. "I'm just going to have to do it for you."

Alex went to grab her breasts, but before he could, Sarah became livid. Her jaw clenched, and her eyes burned in anger. She then jerked her body away from him as much as possible.

"Don't you touch me, you fucking pig!" she cried.

Alex's eyes darkened with anger, and he punched her in the face. Sarah continued to cry. She had never been in so much pain.

Alex then harshly grabbed her chin. "You know what? You need to learn to shut your yap!" he exclaimed. "I would hate to have to gag that pretty little mouth of yours."

"I've got something to gag her mouth with," one attacker said and laughed.

"I think we all have something we can gag her mouth with," said the other.

One of the men behind her grabbed her hair and pulled her head back toward him. She was now staring up at him.

"And you'd better enjoy it, sweetheart!" he ordered, looking down on her. He then shoved her head back, so she was once again facing Alex.

"Tell you what, sweetheart," said Alex. "You go down on each of us, and we'll return the favor. We'll each go down on you. I don't know about you guys, but I can't wait to get my tongue in that sweet little tight virgin pussy. Well, I assume it's virgin pussy. We'll know soon anyway. On your knees, princess."

Sarah's skin began to crawl.

"No!" she cried. *"Please!"*

The two men behind her were fighting to get her to go down to the floor, but she kept struggling against them. The more she struggled, the more they tightened their grip on her.

Sarah kept trying to look toward the front door. She hoped that either her father or her uncle would walk in and rescue her. They didn't. Sarah could only keep crying and begging for mercy.

"I'm begging you!" she cried. "Stop! Please!"

"I said on your knees, bitch!" screamed Alex.

He then let out a maniacal laugh.

He punched her in the stomach, and she fell to the floor. Alex's cohorts grabbed her arms. They then forced her onto her knees. She began crying in horror as Alex started to unbuckle his belt.

"You'd better not try to bite down on my dick!" said Alex angrily. "Or the next thing that's going into your mouth will be my shotgun, and that can go off a lot faster." He then exposed his privates to her. The men behind her were trying to hold her head in place.

"*No*! Please, don't!" she screamed. She kept struggling against them and was trying to keep her mouth closed.

"Scream all you want, baby doll!" Alex laughed. "No one's coming to help you."

But unbeknownst to him, there was indeed someone. Out of pure terror and self-preservation, she panicked. Her survival instincts were now in high gear. Without even thinking and before she even realized it, the words just came screaming out of her mouth. *"Michael! Help me!"*

***

Chapter 13
Her Guardian Demon

In the grand ballroom, Michael was trying to get everything organized for his wedding to Sarah. He handed a piece of paper to his first victim ever, Father Thomas. Father Thomas was a local priest who had performed Pauline and Jason's wedding ceremony. He knew what had really happened to the manor.

The good father tried to exorcise Michael from the manor and free Jason's soul. It was a long shot, but he had to try. However, Father Thomas had failed. He only knew how to exorcise demons from people. Separating a witch's spirit from a house was completely different. An exorcism only worked on demons, not on a witch's ghost.

"These are the vows that you will use during the ceremony," Michael told him.

Father Thomas was appalled by what Michael wanted from him.

"I refuse to have her recite these vows," said Father Thomas. "I will not do anything that will compromise this innocent girl. Why do you want me to perform this sham of a wedding? All you have to do is get her to pledge her eternal soul to you. That I will not help you do!"

"I am not compromising anybody, especially her," Michael replied. "She deserves a beautiful and romantic wedding. I want it to be special for her. It is just one way that I can share my love with her. I don't want her to just pledge her soul to me. I want it to seem like a true marriage. Otherwise, I wouldn't have cared who they were. I would have let you pledge your soul to me that night. Then again, you had an ulterior motive."

"I couldn't exorcise your spirit," said Father Thomas. "So I knew that if I had pledged my soul to you, it would have been my life-force that would complete the void. I would have had the power, not you. Then I could have expelled both you and Jason. Your souls would have been set free, and then both of you would have faced final judgment. I have a pretty good idea were each one of you would have ended up."

"And then you would have been trapped in the void, alone forever," replied Michael. "So I guess it was best for both of us that I stopped you before you even had the chance. No offense, Father, but you're not exactly my type. I don't want just anyone. I will only spend eternity with someone I love. But I need her to give me all the power that she will have once the void is complete. So these wedding vows not only ensure that; they are an expression of beautiful and romantic love."

"There is nothing beautiful, romantic, or loving about these vows! Or this wedding!" exclaimed Father Thomas. "I will never perform this unholy ceremony!"

"You don't have a choice, Father!" Michael replied with anger. "I control all the spirits in this manor, including you. The only one who has to make a freewill choice is Sarah!"

"And how do you plan on getting her to do that, Michael?" asked the angry priest.

"*That*, Father," Michael angrily began, "is none of your concern!"

"Tell me, Michael," Father Thomas said inquisitively. "You've never before been in my mind. Why is that?"

"Maybe I'm afraid of what I might find," Michael snarled back at him. "Are you like some of your brethren? Do you like little girls or little boys?"

"That is disgusting!" exclaimed Father Thomas. "You can't blame a whole church for a few bad priests. No, I have never done that, and I never would."

"Typical Catholic hypocrisy," replied Michael. "Just like when you burned witches to death. How many light witches or non-witches were burned at the stake? Or what about the Spanish Inquisition? How many innocent people died because of the church? Because of God's so-called love?"

"There have been mistakes in the past," Father Thomas responded. "The church has been run by human beings, not God himself. Humans are the most fallible of beings. Just out of curiosity, are you afraid of God, Michael?"

"This is my realm, Father. Here, I am God!" proclaimed Michael. "What has God done for me or for you for that matter? You, a faithful servant of his, have been trapped here for two hundred years! Why hasn't your God come to save you?"

"God always finds a way to bring his children home," replied Father Thomas. "All of us will eventually be free of you. Even if you create your void, he will find a way to bring us all home to him. As for you, I don't know. I am not God; that is not my decision to make. You are lucky that it's not!"

Michael looked at him and then gave him a sarcastic smile. "I've always wondered, Father," he asked, "how did you know what happened that night?"

"I saw the explosion," replied Father Thomas.

"I know that's what you've said before," replied Michael, "and yet I think you're hiding some missing information from me. I could go into your mind to find out what it is. Just what are you hiding from—"

"Michael, help me!"

"Sarah, oh my God, *Sarah*!" yelled Michael. "I hear you! Someone is hurting you! Where are you? Who's hurting you?"

He began to panic. She was in trouble. He had to go find her.

"What's wrong?" asked a frantic Karen. Her spirit had manifested in the ballroom, while Todd's and Jason's were not far behind. Karen had heard Michael cry out in anguish.

"Sarah's in danger because of your worthless husband!" Michael replied in anger. "He was supposed to keep an eye on her!"

Michael concentrated on Sarah's thought and was able to locate her at her uncle's house. "I'm coming, Sarah!" he cried. With that, his spirit left the manor.

***

"I don't believe it," said Jason, with astonishment.

"What?" asked a curious Todd.

"This is the first time I've ever seen him put someone else's needs before his own," replied Jason. "I think he really does love her."

***

"Shut up, you little slut, and suck on it!" screamed Alex as he forced his member into Sarah's mouth.

"Who's Michael?" asked Alex. "Your father, your uncle, or is he your boyfriend?" Again, the three of them began to laugh. Then, suddenly, out of nowhere, a strange cold breeze entered the room. It was the calm right before the storm.

"I am Michael!" a loud, thunderous voice roared.

Then all three men started gasping for air. Michael had stopped their hearts, but his anger for them turned into pure hatred. They were hurting his beloved Sarah. His spirit completely enveloped Sarah, to shield her from harm.

With all his anger, the three hapless, dying men began to levitate. However, Michael was determined to protect his precious Sarah. He didn't want her to witness her assailants' soon-to-be horrific demise. So he covered her eyes and forced her to close them.

He then turned his attention back to her attackers. The three men started having violent convulsions. Their bodies began shaking, and blood poured from their eyes.

Then with one final burst of hatred and anger, their bodies exploded. Blood and flesh splattered throughout the room. Everything in that room was covered in the gory mess—everything, except for Sarah. Michael's spirit had protected her from the fallout.

He gently cradled her in his loving arms. He looked at her, and for the first time in his existence, he felt empathy. If he had had tear ducts, he would have cried.

He saw that her blouse had been ripped open and the bruises to her face and stomach. As his cold fingers lightly caressed her delicate face, he saw her swollen, bloody lip. *How could they hurt her like that?*

He looked into Sarah's mind and was angered by how they had tormented her. His hatred was fueled even more when he saw how they had sullied her mouth. Michael screamed in agony, not just because of his rage. He also experienced both her mental and physical pain as well.

"Sarah, I'm sorry they hurt you," cried Michael. *"I should have kept a better eye on you. But I had too much faith in an incompetent imbecile!"*

***

Sarah looked in the direction of his voice and began to cry. Then she shivered—both from the ordeal and from Michael's presence.

"I'm sorry, my love," he said reassuringly. *"I promise I'll keep you warm."*

Then, to her surprise, a blanket just appeared out of nowhere.

How did he do that? she wondered.

The blanket started to gently wrap around her, like a cocoon. She couldn't see him, but she could feel him holding her in a loving embrace.

Even though she feared him, he was all she had. Sarah needed to feel comforted and loved. So she leaned her head and placed her hand against his spirit, letting him take care of her. She felt warm and safe in his arms. Sarah felt cold lips pressed against her forehead as he gave her a small kiss.

"I love you, Sarah," whispered Michael. *"Don't worry. They're not going to get away with this. They're going to pay. I have them. Their souls belong to me. When I get done with them, they are going to wish they were burning in hell! No one hurts my beloved and gets away with it. No one hurts my angel, my Sarah."*

Sarah looked up toward Michael's general direction. "M-Michael!" she cried.

"What is it, my love?" he asked.

"Please," cried Sarah, "please just hold me. Hold me tight, and don't let me go. I just need to feel safe. Please keep me safe and warm."

"Don't worry, Sarah," replied Michael. *"I love you, and I will always protect you. Once you're forever in my arms, you'll always be safe and warm. I promise I will always take care of you, and I will never let you go!"*

He concentrated on Jonathan. He wanted to get Sarah to the manor. The closer he was to it, the stronger his power. Over time, the manor itself became the source of all his power. And healing pain took a lot more effort than causing it.

He could heal both her physical and emotional wounds once he got her back to the manor. Her memory of the incident could be erased. Michael kept trying to contact Jonathan. However, he seemed to be outside of Michael's perimeter of existence.

Damn it! Where the hell is he? Michael wondered internally. *If I can't sense him, that means he must be out of town. Why? He knew he was supposed to keep an eye on her! Why was he not watching her?*

Sarah kept moaning and crying in pain.

"Relax, Sarah. Go to sleep," he whispered while gently rocking her.

***

As Michael held her in his ghostly arms, she could actually feel his true love for her. He made her feel secure and warm. How could this be the same man? This man she could learn to love but not the sadistic monster. He had hurt so many people, yet she could see he had a gentler side. His gentle rocking and his soothing words soon helped her drift off to sleep.

***

As Michael looked down at her injured but still beautiful face, it was at that moment, he realized he was changing. Sarah brought out something inside of him that he had never before known existed. She had weakened him, and yet at the same time, she had made him stronger. She made him a complete person.

Michael looked toward Evangeline. He noticed that Evangeline was still lying unconscious on the floor. He thought about taking possession of her body and trying to get Sarah to the manor that way. But he knew her body would be limited, especially with what her son had done to her. Plus, she was a medium. Mediums were in contact with other spirits, as well as guardian angels. It was likely he couldn't possess her. She would be too protected.

Sarah was hurt badly and in desperate need of medical attention. He had no choice. He was going to have to call emergency services. This was going to take a lot of effort and concentration on his part. Michael concentrated on the phone lines. He was now able to call for help.

"Nine-one-one, what is your emergency?" the dispatcher asked.

"I'm at 1232 Ocean Drive, the mayor's residence," he told her. "The mayor's niece, Sarah Gilmore, was sexually assaulted by three men. She's in urgent need of medical attention."

"We'll send an ambulance over right away," replied the operator. "Can I have your name and phone number, please?"

"*No,*" he replied, "because I brutally murdered her three rapists. You won't find me—ever!"

"I'm sorry, sir," the shocked dispatcher replied. "Did you just say you brutally murdered them?"

"Yes, now quit wasting my time, and just send help over here!" Michael demanded.

He then cut his link into the phone lines. Michael looked down at his sleeping beauty. He hated seeing her beautiful face injured like that. He wanted to get her to the manor as soon as he could. He could heal all her wounds there. But he was going to have to wait until she was seen by a doctor.

"Just sleep, my love," he whispered. *"I will stay with you until help arrives. You'll be safe in my arms. Then I will take care of that worthless Jonathan. He too shall pay. I can't take you now. If I possessed an ambulance driver, there would be too many people around who could stop me."*

As his sleeping angel remained in his arms, she let out a contented sigh. He looked down at his precious Sarah. She was so beautiful, so innocent, and so loving. She was everything he ever wanted in a wife. Michael then ran his ghostly fingers through her long red hair, and it gave off such an alluring fragrance.

"Don't worry, Sarah," whispered Michael. *"I won't let anyone take what rightfully belongs to me. I'm going to take you away, far from this wretched realm! And you, my dear, will be pampered and want for nothing. I promise to spoil you rotten, if that's even possible. You, my dear Sarah, will be mine forever."*

***

CHAPTER 14
There Can Be Consequences

Robert was at the auto repair garage that Eric had taken him to. He was still waiting for his car to even be towed to the repair garage. While he was waiting, he was able to at least charge his phone.

He kept trying to get hold of Sarah. *Why isn't she answering her phone? Maybe she just fell asleep?* Robert called her cellphone a fifth time.

"Hey, this is Sarah. Please leave a message."

"Hey, Sarah, it's me again," said Robert. "Look, I don't want to come off as the overprotective father, but this is my fifth message. To be honest, I'm starting to get worried. Please call me back as soon as possible."

He kept pacing around the repair shop's lobby, looking at his phone. The woman at the front desk just kept watching him. She was probably worried that he was going to wear a hole in the floor. Robert had a bad feeling. *What if something is wrong?*

Sarah had just recently blossomed. For years, she was the tall, skinny redheaded girl with an overbite. This caused her to wear braces, including the headgear, for three years.

Puberty was extremely difficult, but she got through it. Once she did, her body filled out. The braces did their job and were no longer needed. She was not the same girl she was a year ago.

Robert didn't know how to handle the situation. That should have been Helen's job. Helen was gone at a time when Sarah really needed her mother. Robert feared that Sarah could easily be manipulated by unscrupulous men. Just then, his cellphone rang.

Oh, thank God, he thought. But when he looked at the number, he saw it wasn't Sarah's. It was the police department. Robert's eyes widened, and he began to feel sick to his stomach. He calmed himself down and accepted the call.

"Hello?" he answered fearfully.

"Mr. Gilmore, it's Lieutenant Johnson," said Eric.

"Oh my God, what happened to Sarah?" asked Robert.

***

Jonathan had just returned to his office. He was alone. Guilt was consuming him. How was he going to betray his brother and niece?

No, Karen comes first, he thought. *She's all that matters. Besides, Sarah is not going to be a slave like Karen. Michael is practically going to worship Sarah.* Just then, there was a chill in the room.

"Jonathan," he heard Michael's voice say, *"where is Sarah?"*

"Look, Robert insisted on spending the day with her," said Jonathan. "You're going to take her away from him. I thought they should have this day together."

"Jonathan," said a more annoyed Michael, *"where is Sarah?"*

"I was explaining, she's at my home with her father," replied Jonathan.

"Wrong!" screamed Michael.

With that, Jonathan went flying across the room. He was shocked and in pain, as his body had been thrown against the wall. When he fell to the floor, it took a while for him realize what had just happened. He staggered a bit, as he forced his own aching body to stand up again.

"Sarah is in an ambulance on her way to the hospital!" screamed a furious Michael.

"What do you mean? Why?" asked Jonathan.

"She was gang raped in your home!" yelled Michael. *"By that Evangeline Nelson's son and two other reprobates."*

"What were they doing in my home? Is Sarah okay?" asked Jonathan. Then out of nowhere, what felt like a cold fist hit his face. The force was so powerful, Jonathan hit the floor.

"Did I say you could talk, Jonathan?" asked Michael. *"Get up!"*

At this point, he was beyond angry. He watched as Jonathan struggled to stand once again.

"Evangeline went to see Sarah," Michael began. *"And her repugnant son,*

a serial rapist, and two other lowlifes followed her to your home! They beat up both Evangeline and Sarah! You know how I found out?"

Jonathan didn't respond.

"Answer me!" screamed Michael.

"No, how?" asked Jonathan.

"Sarah called me for help!" explained Michael. *"When I got there, you know what I found, Jonathan? His filthy penis in my angel's mouth! I not only killed them; I destroyed them."*

"Oh my God!" cried Jonathan.

"Quiet, Jonathan! Don't speak unless I tell you to!" exclaimed Michael. *"Now, you may have to sleep somewhere else tonight. Your living room is covered in what's left of their worthless carcasses. I'm not done with them; I have them now. They will know my wrath. I will make their meaningless existences a torturous hell. Now then, Jonathan, do you have a question?"*

"Is Sarah all right?" asked Jonathan.

"As well as can be expected," replied Michael. *"No thanks to you! I guess you want Karen's soul trapped forever! You have failed me for the last time! The deal is off!"*

Tears began to well up in Jonathan's eyes, and he started to cry.

"No!" cried Jonathan. "Please, please give me another chance. I'll do anything."

"Anything? Fine," said Michael. *"I'll give you another chance. However, I'm only giving you one more. Just one more chance! Now I have always tried to behave as a proper gentleman. Even as dark as my soul is, I do not physically harm women. True, I have ended the lives of any woman who tried to have me destroyed—including Karen. But I made their deaths as quick and painless as possible. Even now, I do not cause harm to Karen, or any of the other female spirits trapped in the manor. So help me, Jonathan. If you fail me again, both Karen and Todd will share the same fate as the three men that defiled my Sarah!"*

"No! Please! I'm sorry! I thought Robert was spending the day with her!" cried Jonathan. "Sarah's my niece. I would never want anything bad to happen to her. But punish me, not Karen!"

"No more excuses, you imbecile!" screamed Michael. *"Fortunately, for you, I need you alive. I have a plan. I should have known better than to trust you. I should have done this from the start."*

"What is your plan?" asked Jonathan.

"No!" said Michael. *"I'm not telling you anything! You'll just fail me as you've already done, like earlier today, when you almost warned Robert about me. I was in your mind when I entered this room, before I even spoke to you. You almost betrayed me, didn't you?"*

Jonathan didn't know how or if he should respond.

"Didn't you?" exclaimed Michael.

"I-I'm sorry," replied Jonathan. "I-I had moment of weakness. You have to remember I love my brother, as well as my niece. I just can't stand the thought of hurting them. But I did stop myself. I didn't tell Robert anything. Even though it was difficult, I swear I didn't tell him anything."

"I can't trust you!" exclaimed Michael. *"Not as long as you are unable to figure out your priorities. You're going to have to decide who is more important to you, Robert or Karen. Decide wrong, and it will cost you dearly. When I need you, I'll come to you. When I'm ready, you will know. I am now taking matters into my own hands."*

***

CHAPTER 15
A Father's Anguish

Lieutenant Johnson had sent a patrol car to go pick up Robert from the repair shop. Robert was horrified when he found out about Sarah. It felt as though his heart had literally hit the floor. Tears began to stream down his face like a waterfall.

Dear God! Why? he wondered. *First, you take my wife! Then you let these degenerates hurt my daughter? What has my family done to deserve this?*

On the way to the hospital, he called Jonathan's cell.

Jonathan saw that his brother was calling him, and he already knew why. He just needed to act surprised. He didn't need to act horrified. Jonathan answered his phone.

"Hello?"

"J-J-Jon-athan!" cried Robert.

"Robert, what's wrong?" asked Jonathan.

"Oh my God! Oh my God!" Robert cried. "I can't, I can't even say it!"

Jonathan could hear his poor brother sobbing in agony.

"Robert? Did something happen to Sarah?" asked Jonathan. "What happened to Sarah?"

"She was gang raped by three escaped convicts!" cried Robert. "It's all my fault! I left her alone! Dear God, why did I leave her alone? If I had stayed home, the fucking perverts wouldn't have assaulted my little girl! I hope they burn in hell!"

"Robert, listen to me. It's not your fault," said Jonathan. "You had no way of knowing. Where are you now?"

"I'm in the back of a patrol car, on the way to the hospital," cried Robert.

"Look, Robert, I'm on my way," said Jonathan. Then he hung up the phone.

Shit! thought Jonathan as he got into his car. *Robert, why? Why did you leave her? Oh my God, you have no idea what you have done! Karen may suffer because of you. Wait ... I should've been on top of things. My niece was raped because of me. Sarah and Robert are both in a lot of pain. And I'm going to make it worse. Oh God! Why do I have to do this to them? Why did this have to happen to Karen?*

***

When Robert arrived at the hospital, he ran into the emergency room. He went up to the front desk. He was breathing heavily and in a panic.

"Excuse me!" Robert began. "My—"

"I'll be with you in one moment, sir," said the receptionist abruptly. "I'm on the phone right now."

"Look, lady!" screamed Robert. "I don't give a damn about your hen party! So get your ass off the fucking phone, and tell me where I can find my daughter!"

"Sir, do I have to call security?" she asked firmly.

"Listen!" screamed Robert. "My daughter is back there!"

"Sir!" she began. "I'm going to have to—"

Before she could finish, Lieutenant Johnson interrupted her. He had just entered the emergency room while Robert was having it out with the receptionist.

"It's okay, ma'am," said Eric, showing her his badge. "Let us back there, please." She shot Robert an angry look before letting the automatic doors open. Robert was still crying and began to calm down.

"I'm sorry," cried Robert. "This isn't like me. I'm just so upset right now."

"It's okay," said Eric. "I understand. I would tell you you need to calm down, but I think I would probably act the same way."

"Why? Why Sarah?" asked Robert. "Why her? Oh God! I don't know if I can even face her. She needs me to be strong. I'm going take one look at her, and I won't be able to stop crying. I'm going to be completely useless to her."

"The only thing she needs now is her father," said Eric. "Now, I'm

84

going to have to ask her some questions. These questions will be very uncomfortable for both of you, but it has to be done. Can you handle my asking her these questions? If not, it might be best if you're not in the room. Either way, a female police officer will be on hand. I've also notified a rape counselor. She will be here soon."

"Sarah needs me," said Robert. "Unless she feels uncomfortable about it, I'll stay."

They then proceeded into Sarah's room. The female officer Eric had been referring to was already there. She had been keeping Sarah company, waiting for Robert to arrive.

Robert was not prepared for what he saw. Sarah's cheeks were covered in bruises, and she had a black eye. Her upper lip had a cut on it, and it was swollen. As he looked at her, tears welled up in both of their eyes. He and Sarah burst into tears.

"Daddy," she cried, as her father embraced her.

"Oh, princess!" cried Robert. "I'm so sorry this happened to you. I should have never left you alone."

"Sarah, do you remember me?" Eric asked.

"Yes," she replied with a sad smile and her eyes full of tears.

"Sweetheart," Eric began in a soothing voice, "now it's up to you if you want your father here. I have to ask you some very personal questions. It might be best to have a loved one with you. But I could understand why you might not want him in here. You might not be comfortable answering them in front of him. Now the nice lady that you've been talking to, that's Officer Carolyn Jenkins. Whether or not you want your father in here, Officer Jenkins will stay as moral support. Do you want your father in here?"

"Yes," she answered.

"Okay, Sarah, from the beginning, what happened?" asked Eric.

Sarah then began to recount everything that had happened. Her father's heart sank as she talked about the horrible events.

"Sarah," asked Eric, "was there any form of penetration?"

Sarah's eyes began to tear up again as she gave a confirming nod.

"Where, sweetheart?" asked Eric.

"M-my mouth," she replied in a low, soft voice. She felt ashamed and kept her head down.

Robert tried his best to little or no avail to keep from crying. He then covered his face with both hands and ran them through his hair. He internally screamed in his head.

Oh God, why?

"Was there any other place, Sarah?" Eric asked.

"No," she replied in the same soft voice.

"Do you know which one did it?" asked Eric.

"Alex, Alex Nelson," she told him.

"Okay, honey, Officer Jenkins is going to take a swab of your mouth," Eric told her.

The female officer took a long swab stick and swabbed all along the inside of Sarah's mouth. She caused Sarah to gag a little before she finished.

"Sorry, sweetie," Officer Jenkins said to her with a caring smile. "You did an excellent job." She then placed it in a vial and sealed it up.

"Since the only place was her mouth, I think that's enough for the rape kit," said Eric. "Sarah, do you know who killed them?"

"Yes, but—" she began.

Eric cut her short.

"Look, honey," he began, "I know why you may want to protect this person, but we need to find out who he is. The quicker we find him, the better it will actually be for him."

"Michael, Michael Winworth," she replied. "I know you don't believe me."

"Honey, Michael Winworth's been dead for two hundred years," Robert responded. "Please, you have to tell the Lieutenant the truth."

"But I am, Daddy," she cried. "It's my fault he killed them. I asked for his help. I didn't mean to. I was just so scared. I begged for his help before I even realized it. He killed Todd and Aunt Karen. Daddy, he's after me. He says that if I don't marry him, you'll die like everyone he's ever killed. Mrs. Nelson was able to get me in contact with Mom. She says we have to leave tonight. I'm frightened, Daddy. Please! Don't let him get me! He's going to take me away from you forever! I'll never see you or Mom again!"

"Is that why she was over there?" asked Robert. "Sarah, she's a con artist. If not, then she's crazy. Either way, she did not get you in contact with your mother. Oh my God, she's screwed with your head. No wonder you think a two-hundred-year-old ghost is after you."

"Daddy, he's real!" cried Sarah. "Remember last night, the night terror? Daddy that was him! You have to believe me! We have to leave now, before it's too late!"

She then tried to get out of the bed. Her father grabbed her and tried calming her down while keeping her in bed.

"Whoa! Whoa! Sarah, sweetheart, you're not making any sense," said Robert. "You've been through two extremely horrible experiences in the last couple of days, and you're not thinking straight. Plus, that woman has you confused; she's been messing with your head."

He then turned his attention to Eric.

"I want that woman arrested!" Robert demanded.

"I think it would be best if we discussed that outside," Eric replied. "Officer Jenkins, can you keep Sarah company a while? Her father and I will talk in the hall."

Robert and Eric then left the room.

"Daddy!" screamed Sarah. "Please don't leave me! I'm not crazy! Daddy, we have to leave! You have to believe me! Daddy!"

"It's okay, sweetie. Calm down," said Officer Jenkins. "They'll be right back."

Eric and Robert made their way into the hallway.

"Please arrest that crazy woman," said Robert. He wanted to shorten the conversation as much as possible. He could hear Sarah still crying for him.

"I can't," replied Eric. "She was dead when we found her. The ME's doing an autopsy right now. My guess is it was a brain hemorrhage. She had been hit and kicked in the head."

"Oh my God," said Robert. "What if they'd killed Sarah? No wonder she's having a breakdown."

"Look, obviously your daughter has been through a couple of major traumas in the last couple of days," said Eric. "I don't think she's covering for the killer. I think she may need some psychiatric therapy. You have no idea how the men who attacked Sarah were brutally murdered. I have never seen anything like it."

"What are you talking about?" asked Robert. "I'm not going to pretend that I feel bad for those guys. Whoever it was probably saved Sarah's life."

"You don't understand. Your daughter was right," said Eric. "The three men had indeed exploded. I mean, there is nothing left of them. There is nothing but blood and flesh all over your brother's living room. Evangeline was covered in their blood, but Sarah wasn't. In fact, we didn't find any blood on her. Whoever killed those men did it out of revenge for Sarah. Now I, of course, don't believe the Michael Winworth story. However, there is no logical explanation for any of this. I have five dead bodies in the last two days. Four of those deaths go beyond any logical or scientific explanation. But they all have one common denominator, Sarah."

***

CHAPTER 16
Brotherly Love

"Just what are you implying?" asked Robert.

"Have you noticed that your brother has been acting strange lately?" asked Eric.

"Well, yes, but you have to remember he just lost his wife two months ago," said Robert. "Take it from me; that can be devastating."

"I know, but let me ask you," Eric began, "has he taken an unhealthy interest in your daughter lately? Any signs of being more overly protective than normal?"

"I mean a little, but he's her godfather," said Robert. "He just lost the love of his life. That could make anyone be a little more overprotective of loved ones. He hasn't seen Sarah in over a year. He was still expecting to see a shy, awkward girl. I think her appearance took him by surprise."

"That's exactly my point," said Eric. "He wasn't expecting a beautiful young woman."

"Look," said Robert, "you have been more than kind to Sarah and me. I am truly grateful, but I cannot believe what you are hinting at. My brother loves Sarah, but only as a niece. I mean, I can't believe what you're saying."

"Listen, I don't think Jonathan Gilmore has an obsession with Sarah," said Eric. "But watching your thirty-eight-year-old wife drop dead of a heart attack could cause a severe mental breakdown. Sometimes the human psyche can't handle these situations, and trauma could lead to the development of a dual identity."

"What are you, a psychiatrist now?" asked an annoyed Robert.

"No, but I've been on the force for a little over twenty years," said Eric.

"Most of those years were with the NYPD. Let's just say I've seen a lot of cases where even sudden mental trauma can negatively affect the mind. Now, you said that your wife died six months ago, but he hasn't seen Sarah in a year. Why didn't he attend your wife's funeral?"

"Because he was just inaugurated as the mayor; he couldn't just take off," Robert replied. "Look, this is crazy. My brother doesn't have a mental disorder, let alone a dual identity."

"Did your brother ever have feelings for your late wife, and does Sarah resemble her in any way?" asked Eric.

"Not that it's any of your business," replied Robert, "but yes, Sarah resembles her mother. Yes, Helen and Jonathan dated before in high school, and yes, she broke his heart. Then Helen and I started dating a couple of years later. He was angry at both of us for a while, but then he met Karen. He absolutely adored her. In fact, Karen was the one who convinced us all to get over any previously hurt feelings."

"It's just starting to fit a profile," said Eric. "I know your brother loved his late wife, but his feelings for your late wife perhaps never completely went away."

"I can assure you that Jonathan's feelings toward Helen were completely platonic!" replied Robert. He couldn't believe what the lieutenant was saying.

"All I know is that these four strange deaths revolved around both Sarah and Jonathan," said Eric. "The murders of the three men were at his house. Also, his brother-in-law died while on a date with Sarah. Your brother just happened to show up soon afterward. He was also quite nervous when I asked him about it."

"First of all," Robert began, "they were not on a date. I mean, Todd was thirty. I wouldn't let him date my sixteen-year-old daughter. Second, Jonathan's the mayor. Was it really that unusual for him to be downtown? Third, of course he was nervous. His wife and her brother had just died unexpectedly in a two-month period. Why are you so suspicious of my brother?"

"Okay, this has already been in the papers," explained Eric, "so I'm not going to tell you anything that the rest of the public doesn't already know. Jonathan has been under investigation for the last six weeks. There have been accusations of mishandled city funds. There has also been some evidence that Jonathan may have laundered ten thousand dollars from the city's treasury."

"What sort of evidence?" asked Robert. "Do you realize what you're accusing my brother of?"

"Those are the details that I cannot go into," said Eric.

"This is crazy. What you're saying about my brother, it's insane. He would never do this. On top of that, you believe he wants Sarah. She's my daughter; he's my brother. They're blood relatives."

"Your daughter said that Michael Winworth raped her last night, even though she was dreaming," said Eric. "There have been cases where a woman has dreamed that she was raped. She swears it felt too real to not have actually happened. It is then later found that she was raped while she was asleep."

Robert's anger was starting to build up inside of him. As his heart began to race, he clenched both his jaw and his fists. Robert was not a violent man, but if Eric hadn't been an officer of the law, he probably would have decked him.

"Wait!" exclaimed Robert. "You think my brother raped my daughter? How can you make that accusation? Jonathan would never, I mean *never*, hurt Sarah."

"Again, I don't think Jonathan would either," said Eric. "But if he took on a dual personality, that other personality might. Maybe it could be because of the superstition surrounding the manor and the way Karen died so suddenly. If he has a dual personality, maybe his other personality is Michael Winworth. Your daughter is so traumatized right now, he could have easily convinced her that he actually is Michael Winworth."

Robert sighed in frustration.

"You know what, Lieutenant?" said Robert. "You have no right to diagnose my brother with anything! You are neither a doctor nor a psychiatrist. Now, I could stand here and angrily defend my brother all day. But, you see, I can't do that right now! I have a sixteen-year-old daughter in the ER! She needs me right now!"

"Listen, Mr. Gilmore—" Eric started to say.

"No, you listen!" Robert exclaimed. "I don't have time for nonsense! By the way, I hope you don't find the guy who killed them. I don't care what the hell he did to them! As far as I'm concerned, he's a hero, not a murderer! Now, I think it might be best if you leave! If there's anyone who seems to have an unhealthy obsession with my daughter, it's you!"

Robert gave Eric an angry stare, before turning to walk away. As he headed back to Sarah, he ran into Jonathan, who was coming down the hallway.

"I'm so sorry this happened to Sarah!" Jonathan cried, embracing his brother. "How is she?"

"As good as can be expected, I assume," replied Robert. "That seems to be the normal answer about her well-being these days."

"Are there any leads on who killed her attackers?" asked Jonathan.

"Not yet, but I—" Robert began. "Jonathan, how did you know the attackers were killed?"

"Um, you-you told me over the phone. Remember?" replied Jonathan. "You know, you were under a lot of stress when you called. I mean, how else could I possibly have known that?"

"Huh?" said Robert. "I just don't remember telling you that. Oh well, I guess I just forgot."

***

CHAPTER 17
Just Another Day at the Beach

Robert and Jonathan headed for Sarah's room. Although Robert was still angry at Lieutenant Johnson, the veteran officer had put doubts into his head. No, not his own brother. Although, for years, he had suspected that a part of Jonathan never really got over Helen. Even if that were true, he would never mistake Sarah for Helen. Would he?

"Oh my God!" Jonathan said when he looked at Sarah. He walked over to her, and she started to cry.

"Uncle Jon, I am so sorry," cried Sarah, as she threw her arms around him.

"For what, sweetie?" asked Jonathan.

"The men who attacked me, it's my fault how they died," she replied. "Your living room is going to need a lot of work. They just exploded."

"Listen, Sarah," said Jonathan. "I'm sure it's not your fault. Even if it was your fault, rooms can be fixed. All I care about is that you're safe."

A nurse entered the room.

"We have a bed available now," she said and smiled. "It's a private room, with a sofa. If you want, your father may stay with you tonight."

"Well, I would like that very much," said Robert. "Besides, the police aren't letting anyone into Jonathan's house right now. It'll save me money on a hotel. Where are you staying, Jon?"

"I have a hide-a-bed in my office," replied Jonathan. "I can sleep there and then shower at the gym."

"Well, great," said the nurse. "The orderlies will take Miss Gilmore to her room then."

The two orderlies released the wheel locks on the bed and moved Sarah toward the elevator. After a short elevator ride, they soon arrived at Sarah's hospital room. Soon afterward, the rape counselor showed up. She lightly knocked on the door.

"Hello, my name is Mimi Anderson," she said and smiled as she walked into the room. "I'm here to help counsel Sarah."

"Oh, please come in," said Robert. "I'm Sarah's father, Robert Gilmore. And this is my brother, Jonathan."

"Of course," said Mimi. "Mayor Gilmore, Robert, and Sarah, it's nice to meet you. May I talk to you gentlemen outside for a second?"

Robert and Jonathan left the room with Mimi.

"Thank you so much for coming," said Robert. "I have to warn you, she's a little delusional right now. She thinks she's being stalked by a ghost."

"Under the circumstances," said Mimi, "a breakdown of some sort isn't that unusual. Look, I know you probably want to stay for my session with her. But it would be best if it was just Sarah and me. She will be more likely to open up to me."

"I understand completely," said Robert. "Besides, Jon and I need to get to a store. We'll need supplies for tonight. Please, help her."

"I will do all I can," said Mimi, "but my guess is she will need long-term therapy."

"I know," replied Robert. He then stuck his head back into the room. "Sweetheart, you and Mimi are going to have a chat for a while. So your uncle and I are going to pick up supplies for tonight."

"No, Daddy!" cried Sarah. "Don't leave me! He's coming for me! Don't let him take me! I'll never see you again!"

Robert walked over to his daughter and gently placed his hands on her face. He looked her square in the eyes.

"It's okay, Sarah," he told her. "This nice woman is here to help you. I will be back later. Remember the locket I gave you. Always keep it with you. As long as you wear it, it will remind you how much I love you. Sweetheart, as long as you know that, no one can ever separate us! Okay?"

She looked at him, nodded, and smiled. He then kissed her forehead.

"I love you, princess," replied Robert. "I'll be back soon. I promise. Let's go, Jonathan."

With that, they left Sarah with the counselor.

"I hope she can help Sarah," said Jonathan. "I know the—"

"Jonathan," said Robert, interrupting him, "we need to talk."

***

Sarah talked to the counselor for an hour, but it didn't help her much. The counselor wanted to talk about Alex Nelson, but Sarah just wanted to talk about Michael Winworth. Mimi was concerned about Sarah having a nervous breakdown. If that was the case, a doctor would likely order some sort of hospitalization.

After a while, Sarah became tired and fell asleep. Mimi thought it would be ideal to just let the poor girl rest. After all, Sarah had been through an extremely traumatic situation. No one had even told Sarah that Evangeline hadn't survived the attack. They weren't sure if she could handle it yet. Mimi left the sleeping girl her business card on the nightstand. On the back, she had written a note.

Please call me if you need me.
—Mimi

As Sarah drifted off further into sleep, she could hear him calling for her.

"Sarah! Sarah! Soon, my love! We will be together forever, and you will be forever mine!"

Sarah soon woke up with a startled gasp, only to find she was not in the hospital room. She was back lying on the beach. She had returned to the Amalfi Coast. It was the exact same beach he had taken her to previously.

She became frightened. Just like before, she was totally aware that she was awake and in her own unconscious mind. She then realized he was standing next to her.

"Hello, my love," said Michael as he slowly lay down next to her. "I just came for a visit. I just want to make sure you're okay. Nobody hurts my angel, my Sarah, and gets away with it."

They were dressed just like they had been when he took her there the first time. He gently stroked her cheek with the back of his finger. She became frightened.

"I-I am not your Sarah," she replied. She tried to act brave, but she began trembling a little.

"Oh?" he responded. "Then why did you call for my help when those degenerates were attacking you? Why did you cry in my arms and then seek my comfort?"

"I was scared," she replied. "I reacted without thinking. It was just survival instinct."

"Maybe calling for me was just instinct," he responded. "Even if it was *just instinct*, you knew the truth. You knew that I was the only one who could save you. Deep down, you know that I am the only one who can love and protect you."

"That's not true!" she protested. "My father loves and protects me."

"But he didn't, did he?" replied Michael. "He left you alone. The truth is, Sarah, all daughters eventually have to leave the comfort of their fathers. It's a dangerous world out there. There are a lot of unscrupulous men who will want to take advantage of you. A combination of beauty, naiveté, and empathy are what make you so special. But it also means that you are too vulnerable. You make a pleasing target, a beautiful woman who can be easily manipulated."

He looked down at her locket. It was so important to her that it had made its way into her unconscious mind. It was obviously precious to her. Otherwise it would not have come with her into her unconscious state.

"When did you get that?" he asked, pointing to it.

"My father gave it to me this morning," she answered. "It is now the most precious thing I own. As long as I wear it, I will always know how much he loves me. And no one can tear us apart."

"May I see it?" he asked. "Don't worry. You can keep it around your neck. I'm not going try to remove it. This is only a dream. It wouldn't matter anyway, but I don't want to upset you."

"Okay," she said with reluctance. However, she wanted him to know just how much she loved her father. The locket was a perfect symbol of that. He gently took it in his hands.

"Sarah, always in our hearts," he read aloud. Then he opened the locket. "Your mother was beautiful, like you. It must be nice to know what it's like to have your parents love you. But your mother's gone, Sarah, and you father can't protect you forever. Only I can do that. You are mine and only mine. I protect any and all belongings that I cherish. You, Sarah, belong to me. You, I will always cherish."

"You want to take me away from my father!" she cried.

"All birds eventually leave their nest," he replied.

"I'm not a bird!" she replied. "I shouldn't have to give up my family."

"Sarah, family members eventually die," he told her. "It's a hard fact of life. Eventually, death would separate you and your father. You will eventually be separated forever. Even if I was willing to let you go, death would come for one of you. All relationships end in heartbreak. You know this reality. It already claimed your mother. Just like it claimed Evangeline."

"No!" she cried. "Please tell me that's not true!"

"It's a sad reality of this cruel world," he told her. "Her own son beat her to death. If you hadn't called me for help, he would have killed you too. You saw their faces; you could've identified them. They weren't going to let you live."

Sarah began to cry, and Michael slowly embraced her. Again, needing a shoulder to cry on, she accepted his loving embrace. It was easy to let him love her. She cared for the person who loved her as much as he did. But she hated the monster he was to everybody else. Realizing this, she pushed him away.

"You've hurt so many people!" she cried. "People I love! You've already threatened my father's life. You said you would stop his heart if I didn't marry you! How can you expect me to love you?"

"I don't want to hurt your father, Sarah," he responded. "He's halfway responsible for your very existence. But I love you! I have never felt this way before. I thought I loved my brother's wife. I was wrong. I can't and I won't let you go. You will be mine! Once we're married, I will become corporeal. You will learn to love me. Then, on our wedding night, I will make you forever mine. Unlike all relationships, ours will not end in heartbreak. We will love each other forever. Do you understand?"

"Yes, you plan on raping me on our so-called wedding night!" she exclaimed. "Just like you did before! Except this time, it won't just be in my unconscious mind! This time, it will be real!"

"Sarah," he responded, "it's true that I took advantage of the fact that I could manipulate your body. You enjoyed the way I orally pleased you to the point of ecstasy. I enjoyed every minute of our lovemaking, as did you. True, I did need to use your libido to experience my own sexual pleasure.

But I couldn't have done it if I did anything you didn't want to do. That's why I didn't have you orally pleasure me. It wouldn't have worked."

"How-how did you know what I wanted?" she asked.

"Don't forget, my dear. I was in your mind. I knew all your secret hidden fantasies. You wanted to be sexually dominated on a beach at sunset. That's what I gave you. That included the one thing you would never admit to secretly desiring, not even to yourself. You wanted a man's tongue to explore your virgin core, while you lay there helpless. Like it or not, my dear, you enjoyed every minute of it. I know because I enjoyed every second."

"Please," she begged, "just let me sleep in peace."

"Fine, I understand," he responded. "You have had a horrific day. I will let you rest. Just know this, the next time I see you, it will be the beginning of our forever. But before I go ..." He then slowly cocked his head to one side and leaned in for a passionate kiss. She did not resist. In fact, she kissed him back. He gave her a pleased smirk. With that, he bent down and kissed her hand.

"Until we see each other again, my love," he said with a wicked smile.

Again, she woke up with a gasp. She was surrounded by the noise of blinking monitors and four white walls. She was back in the cold and dreary hospital room. Where was her father?

Sarah was now more frightened than ever, not just because she knew he was coming for her, but because he didn't have to manipulate her into reciprocating his passion.

***

CHAPTER 18
Things Aren't Always as They Seem

Eric had returned to the police station. He went over the ME's autopsy reports of the five victims. Evangeline's was pretty cut and dry, a brain hemorrhage. That, he had already figured out. She had been kicked in the head. The other four were not so clear. The reports had little to no explanation. Todd's heart and lungs had exploded. There was no evidence of any kind of an accelerant, but there was no known natural cause.

At least Todd had a body. Sarah's three assailants were obliterated. Again, there was no known natural cause and no form of an accelerant found. There wasn't even anything left to identify the bodies. Some of the officers had become sick when they saw the aftermath.

The only evidence they had, besides Sarah's identification of Alex Nelson, was the DNA sample taken from her mouth. That report still hadn't come back from the lab yet. But he was sure results would prove that of whatever was left of the bodies, at least some of it was Alex. A voice analysis expert had gone over the 911 call. He had called back rather quickly.

"Please," said Eric, "tell me the reason you were able to finish your analysis so quickly is because you have some good news."

"I wish I could, Lieutenant," he replied.

"Let me guess," replied Eric. "You can't analyze the murderer's voice. Is there something wrong with the tape?"

"No," he replied. "That's what's odd. There's nothing wrong with the tape."

"What do you mean?" asked Eric, "I don't understand."

"Do you have a copy of it?" he asked Eric.

"Yes, I have a copy right here," said Eric.

"I think you'll have to hear it for yourself," he said.

"Fine," replied Eric. "But I'm keeping you on the line." He listened to the recording.

"Nine-one-one, what is your emergency?"

Long pause.

"We'll send and ambulance over right away."

Long pause.

"Can I have your name and phone number please."

Long pause.

"I'm sorry, sir. Did you just say you brutally murdered them?"

"What the hell!" exclaimed Eric. "Why can't you hear the caller's voice?"

"I don't know," said the expert. "I've listened to that tape over a dozen times. There's nothing wrong with it. It's as if the caller doesn't even exist."

"This is driving me nuts. I have no evidence. Thanks anyway," Eric said and hung up the phone. "Jenkins! Get me through to the dispatcher who took the nine-one-one call on the Gilmore case."

"Right away, sir." She soon patched the dispatcher through to Eric.

"Hello," said Eric, "are you the dispatcher who talked to the man who reported Sarah Gilmore's rape?"

"Yes, I am, sir," she replied.

"Besides confessing to triple homicide, was there anything else peculiar about the call?" Eric asked.

"Well, this is going to sound crazy," she began, "but after I got over the shock of what he said to me, well …"

"Well, what?" Eric asked impatiently.

"Look," she began, "I can't explain it. It was as if … it was as if—"

"It was as if what?" asked Eric, now obviously frustrated. "I don't care how odd it sounds. Just tell me what was so damn strange about it!"

"I swear the voice wasn't on the phone," she replied. "It was as if it were in my head … Sir? Hello?"

He didn't even reply. It was just too unbelievable. Without thinking or caring how rude it was, he just hung up the phone.

"What in the hell is going on?" he said to himself. "I have to get out of this nutty town."

***

Jonathan and Robert headed toward Jonathan's car. As they walked through the emergency room parking lot, Robert just kept looking at his brother. Jonathan was sweating profusely and had what seemed like a nervous look upon his face.

Just what is he hiding? Robert wondered. *Is Eric right? Did he steal $10,000 from the city? Did Karen's death push him over the edge? Has he become obsessed with both Helen and Sarah?*

Jonathan unlocked the doors and let them both into the car. As they drove away, Jonathan turned to Robert.

"Okay," said Jonathan, "what do we need to talk about?"

"Jon," Robert began, "Lieutenant Johnson and I had an interesting conversation about you."

"Let me guess," replied Jonathan. "He told you about the investigation."

"So you know?" asked Robert.

"Yes," said Jonathan. "They've already had me in for questioning. Besides, the whole town knows."

"Jonathan, what the hell is going on?" asked Robert.

"I'm not allowed to discuss it without my attorney present," Jonathan replied.

"Oh, don't give me that bullshit!" exclaimed Robert. "I'm your brother. If you needed help, why didn't you come to me?"

"Why are you so quick to assume I'm guilty?" asked Jonathan.

"I'm not," said Robert. "But you have been acting strange lately. I know that something else is going on besides losing Karen. Now what is it?"

"Nothing is going on, Robert," said Jonathan. "Please just drop it. It's my problem not yours. I'm dealing with it."

"Why are you being accused of stealing ten thousand dollars in city funds?" asked Robert.

"Boy that lieutenant sure has a big mouth, doesn't he?" said Jonathan. "Fine, I was afraid what would happen if the resort deal fell through. I knew that you could lose your shirt if it didn't come to pass. After we failed to get that manor torn down, I felt like I was responsible for suggesting it to you in the first place."

"What does that have to do with anything?" asked Robert.

"I thought if I could get the historical department from the women's college involved, then the manor could eventually become a tourist attraction. Then the resort would have a better chance of being built. So I offered the college's historical department ten thousand dollars."

"What? Why?" asked Robert.

"In exchange, the students would learn about the history of the manor," replied Jonathan. "The historical department would also bring students here to study its exterior structure. I thought I could use funds from the treasury, since it was for the betterment of the town. But apparently the state auditor general doesn't agree with me."

"Oh come on, Jon. You know better than that!" exclaimed Robert.

"Maybe, but I felt desperate," replied Jonathan. "I couldn't protect Karen. I wasn't going to let anything happen to you. You and Sarah had already been through so much after Helen's death."

"Wait!" said Robert. "First of all, Karen died of a heart attack. True, it was odd for a woman her age, but you couldn't have stopped it. Second, are you saying you broke the law because you thought you could protect me?"

"I guess it felt like I failed her," said Jonathan. "I know that I took a big risk in what I did, but I felt like I had no choice. Sometimes you have to do things for the ones you love. You wouldn't believe what someone might be willing to do or even who they are willing to betray."

"Jonathan!" Robert yelled. "Do you understand the severity of this situation? Do you understand that you can go to jail for this?"

"Listen, I can make a plea bargain of some kind," said Jonathan. "I'll have to resign as mayor, but I just don't care anymore anyway. Robert, I know you're concerned about me. I will do whatever has to be done. You don't need to worry about me. Okay? Now, the only person you need to be concerned about is Sarah."

"Fine," replied Robert. "We won't dwell on it, if that's the way you feel."

"Good, thank you," said Jonathan. "Listen, before we run to the drugstore for toiletries, I need to run by my office. Do you need to use the bathroom?"

"That would probably be a good idea," said Robert.

Soon afterward, Jonathan drove them to city hall. He took his keys, opened the door, and let Robert and himself into the building.

Robert was amazed. His little brother was in charge of an entire town. Sure, it was a small town, but it was still an accomplishment. As he and Jonathan continued to walk down the dark and empty hallway, Robert could hear only the echoes of their steps along the tiled floor. The whole experience was almost too surreal.

Robert remembered the night Jonathan called. He was thrilled that his baby brother had won the election. Helen was excited, and Karen was so proud of her husband. A year ago, everything seemed perfect. Now, it seemed like everything was going to hell in a hand basket.

"The bathroom's down the hall and to your right," said Jonathan, pointing. "I won't be in my office long."

Robert went in and used the bathroom. As he began washing his hands, he had a strange feeling. He couldn't explain it. But for some reason, he had an ominous sense of dread.

Then, all of a sudden, he began to feel a cold breeze in the bathroom. He soon thought he heard faint echoes. Then it felt as though someone was behind him. Was he being watched? Robert quickly turned around but saw no one.

What the hell? he thought. *Now I think I'm losing my mind, like the rest of this town.* Robert felt a cold tap on his shoulder.

"Excuse me!" said a haunting male voice. *"I think it's about time we met. After all, we're going to be family soon!"*

Robert let out a loud gasp.

***

Jonathan was finishing up in his office. He had what he needed. Just then, Robert was standing in the frame of the door.

"Well, you were in there a long time," said Jonathan. "You didn't fall in, did you?"

Robert didn't say anything.

Jonathan looked at Robert's face. Jonathan couldn't help but notice that something wasn't quite right about his brother.

Robert had been staring at his own hands with a smug expression on his face.

"You know," said Robert, "it's been a long time since I've been corporeal. I'd forgotten what it felt like."

Jonathan's pulse began to heavily increase, it was at that moment that he realized what was actually happening.

"Michael?" asked Jonathan. "Is that you?"

"Yes," said Michael.

"Oh my God!" cried a stunned Jonathan. "Where's Robert?"

"He's here," said Michael as he placed two finger against his temple. "He's just a little dormant right now, but he's safe. The only thing is, we know each other's thoughts. So he knows about the little arrangement between you and me. I should warn you; he's not very happy with you. Oh well, he'll just have to get over it."

"Why are you in his body?" asked Jonathan timidly.

"I told you that I was going to have to take matters into my own hands," replied Michael while still looking at Robert's hands. "Oh? I guess you didn't realize that I meant it literally. It's time, Jonathan! We're going to bring her home, where she rightfully belongs—with me. Now then, let's go get my baby girl."

***

CHAPTER 19

Out of the Frying Pan and into the Fire

"Sarah whatever you do, as hard as this is going to be for you to except, you can't trust—"

Bang!

"Hello, Mother! Didn't you miss your little boy?"

"Well, well, well, look what we have here. Aren't you just the sweetest little thing? What's your name, princess?"

"I asked you a question, princess. What's your name?"

"Am I making you cry? Because my friends and I can make you feel real good."

"Do we make you scared, Sarah?"

"Do we, baby? I bet we do, and I bet it's just turning you on."

"Those little panties of yours must be soaking wet by now."

"On your knees, princess!"

"Shut up, you little slut, and suck on it!"

"And you'd better enjoy it, sweetheart!"

"Who's Michael? Your daddy?"

"I am Michael!"

Sarah woke up with a gasp and turned on the light. She saw that she was still in the hospital room. Where exactly was her father, and why wasn't he here yet? She was now too frightened to go back to sleep. It was not just fear from reliving the gang rape but from the thought of Michael entering her dreams again.

Then there was her mother's warning. Her mom's spirit was trying to warn her not to trust someone, but whom? Sarah's spiritual link with her mother had been severed when Alex shot the lock off the front door. Her mother never had a chance to tell her whom she shouldn't trust. Sarah was scared and confused and had no idea what to do.

She had never before felt so alone and thought about ringing for the nurse. But what could they do? They had work to do and other patients in their care. She wasn't the only one. If anything, they might give her a sleeping pill. That was the last thing she needed.

She went to use the bathroom. Her body was aching from being punched by Alex in the abdomen. As she washed her hands, she looked in the mirror. It was the first time she'd had a good look at her face since the attack.

Her face looked horrible. Her cheeks were bruised and swollen, while her upper lip had to have stitches. Alex had also given her a black eye and a couple of cracked ribs. But the physical pain was no match for her mental anguish. Her attackers had not only physically hurt her; they had humiliated her. She began to cry.

She couldn't help but feel guilty. Although Michael had shielded her from witnessing the actual ultimate demise of her attackers, she had still seen the aftermath. Sarah had never seen such a horrific display. No one should ever have to suffer like that, not even them. And yet, after what they had done to her, it did feel like some form of justice. She didn't even know how she was supposed to feel.

Why can't we just go home? she thought. *I want things back to normal. I don't want to be violated. I don't want to witness any more people dying, and I don't want to be stalked by a ghost.*

When her mother died, she couldn't imagine how life could get any worse. Unfortunately, now she knew that it could. Sarah made her way back to the bed. It was then that she noticed Mimi's business card.

"Please call me if you need me. Mimi," she read.

Sarah's cellphone was still back at her uncle's house, so she used the phone in her room. She hoped she wasn't calling too late. She dialed the number, and the phone began to ring. She then heard the phone being picked up on the other end.

"Hello?" said Mimi.

"I'm sorry to bother you, Mrs. Anderson," said Sarah. "I'm just scared. My father isn't here yet, and I didn't know where else to turn."

"Don't apologize. That's why I gave you my number," Mimi replied. "Do you need to talk? And please, call me Mimi."

"Yes, I do need to talk," replied Sarah. "I keep having nightmares. I just keep reliving it. I feel so helpless, but at the same time, I feel guilty." She began to cry.

"Sarah, a lot of victims feel guilty," replied Mimi. "But, sweetie, the assault was not your fault. You didn't do anything to deserve being violated like that."

"But their deaths were my fault," cried Sarah. "I called for his help. I didn't know what else to do. He killed them! He scares me, but I am starting to have feelings for him. He's a cruel, sadistic monster, and yet he shows a loving and gentle side toward me—but only me. I hate him, but a part of me longs to be with him. What's wrong with me?"

"Nothing. It sounds to me like Stockholm syndrome," replied Mimi. "But, Sarah, who are you talking about?"

"Michael Winworth," Sarah replied. "I know you don't believe me."

"Sarah, it's not that I don't believe you," said Mimi. "I just think that everything you've been through in the last two days has altered your perception of reality."

"I swear, this isn't all in my head!" cried Sarah. "I'm telling you the truth."

"I'm not saying that these things aren't happening to you. I think it's a real person in your life, whom you care about. But your mind can't handle the fact that a loved one is hurting you. So your mind creates a persona of another predator. Don't you see? The real perpetrator is someone you love and trust. This may be what is leading to your confusion. Sarah, who's really hurting you?"

"I just told you," replied Sarah. "It's Michael Winworth. I'm not crazy."

"I didn't say you are," said Mimi. "I just think you're confused right now. With what you've been through, I would think you were crazy if you didn't have misperceptions of reality."

"I'm not—" Sarah began.

"Sarah!" yelled Robert.

Sarah still had the phone receiver up to her ear.

"Daddy?" cried Sarah. "My father's here. He's coming down the hall. Mimi, I need to go."

"Wait, Sarah!" said Mimi. "Don't hang up the phone. I need to talk to him."

"Okay," said Sarah. She laid the phone receiver on the nightstand and got out of bed to greet him. As soon as he walked into the room, she threw her arms around him. She began to cry.

"Daddy, I'm so glad you're here!" she cried.

He wrapped his arms around her in a loving embrace. She looked up at him and smiled. He smiled back and with one hand, gently caressed her face.

"My beautiful Sarah," he said. He gazed upon her with a loving smile.

"Daddy, please listen to me!" she exclaimed. "We have to leave now. We have to go home!"

"That's why I'm here," he replied. "To take you home with me. I promise you, my dear Sarah, no one will ever harm you again." He looked at her and smiled.

She smiled back with tears in her eyes. She was happy he was going to take her somewhere safe. Again, he gently caressed her cheek.

"You're so beautiful, Sarah," he told her. "So lovely, so delicate—" At that moment, he started to lean in for a passionate kiss.

"Daddy! What are you doing?" she screamed, and she began to struggle against his hold.

"I'm sorry, Sarah," he replied. "I just missed you so much. I wasn't thinking, princess."

Sarah wasn't buying it. She just kept staring at him, right into his green eyes. Those eyes, they were different. They didn't actually look different, but it was the way his eyes were staring at her. All of a sudden, it dawned on her as to what was happening.

"Oh my God!" she cried. "You're not my father! What have you done with … Where is my father?"

"Sarah?" cried Mimi. "Sarah, what's happening? What's going on? Sarah? *Sarah!*"

Michael heard Mimi's voice through the receiver. He looked over at the phone. With just a wave of his hand, he was able to sever the phone connection.

***

As Mimi heard the phone click off, she began to panic. What the hell was going on over there? She called Lieutenant Johnson. She knew he would be in bed, but he was going to want to know what had happened.

"Hello?" said Eric, sounding rather groggy and annoyed.

"Eric, it's Mimi!" she said. "You need to get down to the hospital right away!"

"What's wrong?" he asked.

"It's Sarah Gilmore!" she replied. "She's in a lot of danger! Only it isn't her uncle who's been violating her; it's her father!"

***

CHAPTER 20
Whom Can You Trust?

Sarah was terrified. She realized that Michael had taken possession of her father's body. With fear in her eyes, she slowly backed away from him.

"What have you done with my father?" she cried. He came toward her and smiled at her. With his right hand, he lightly ran his fingers through her hair.

"He's here, Sarah. He's safe," Michael responded. "As long as you cooperate, no harm shall come to him."

"Why? Why are you doing this?" she asked in tears.

He then cupped both sides of her face with his hands. Michael stared into her eyes. As he lightly held her face in his hands, he caressed her cheeks with his thumbs. He could tell by the hypnotized look upon her face that Sarah was slowly beginning to bend to his will.

"You know why, Sarah," he responded. "We belong together. You are mine and only mine. This was inevitable. You knew I was coming for you. No one was going to stand in my way—not Todd, not Alex, not even your father. You never belonged to any of them; you belong to me. Now, if you're good and cooperate, your father won't have to share the same fate. If you don't, well, I'm afraid that he's the one who'll pay for it. You know I will never harm you. Now, Sarah—"

Suddenly, he looked as though he was beginning to struggle. His entire body started to tremble, and his eyes tightly closed shut. For just a short while, Robert was able to regain control over his body.

"S-S-Sarah, r-r-run!" her actual father yelled, snapping Sarah out of her trance.

As both identities struggled for control over Robert's body, Sarah ran out of the room. As she ran down the hall, she saw nurses and other night staff lying motionless on the floor. Upon seeing them she let out a horrified gasp.

"Sarah! Come back here!" she heard her father yell.

It was her father's voice, but through his tone and demeanor, she knew Michael had regained control.

"You know you can't hide from me, Sarah!" exclaimed Michael. "I love you! And I'm never letting you go! The sooner you accept that, the easier it will be on all of us!"

Sarah franticly began pushing elevator buttons and tried opening stairwell doors. But the elevators would just pass the floor, and the stairwell doors were also jammed shut. Was he using his powers to do this?

"Sarah!" he continued to yell.

Not knowing what to do, she hid behind the nurses' station. Sarah began to cry. What was she going to do? Again, she was afraid for her father; she didn't want him to die. But she also feared the idea of Michael keeping her forever. As she stayed there, she held her knees to her chest. Fear and uncertainty were causing her to continue crying.

It was at that moment that she heard one of the elevator doors open. She looked up from behind the nurses' station and saw her uncle getting off the elevator. He stood there and kept looking around.

Oh, thank God! she thought. *But how did he get the elevator door to open, and where did he come from?* It didn't matter. She knew her uncle would protect her. Plus, now they had a means of escape.

She slowly got up and tried to get his attention.

"Uncle Jon," she whispered.

He looked over and saw her. She motioned for him to come to her, and he complied.

"Sarah, what are you doing out of your room?" he whispered back.

"Uncle Jon," she cried, "Michael has taken possession of Daddy. I know you won't believe me, but it's true. You have to help me get out of here. We're in danger if we stay. Come on! We have to go now!"

As she began to try to flee, her uncle grabbed her. Sarah was puzzled but then just figured that he must have thought she was completely out of her mind. She decided that for their own sakes, she had to prove to him otherwise.

"I know it sounds crazy," she told him, "but trust me—we have to go!"

Again, he held her in place. Why wasn't he letting her go? Why wouldn't he let her run? Something was wrong. She just kept looking at his emotionless stare.

"Well, Jonathan! I'm glad to see you finally did something right!" exclaimed Michael. "It seems that hiding you in an elevator as a backup plan worked."

Sarah didn't turn around to look at Michael. She kept her eyes on Jonathan. It was unfathomable to her. How could he betray her?

Jonathan then looked down at her. He had both tears and sorrow in his eyes.

"I'm sorry, Sarah," Jonathan explained. "I didn't have a choice."

She just kept looking at him in disbelief. Tears welled up in her eyes and began to stream down her face. She just kept shaking her head.

"No! No! It can't be!" she cried. "It was you? You were the one that Mom was trying to warn me about? You were the one she said not to trust? I can't believe it's you! I thought you loved me."

"I do, Sarah!" Jonathan cried. "But I love your aunt Karen more. Her soul's trapped in that house. Helping him was the only way that I could get him to release her soul. Sarah, I—"

"I don't want you to get too cold, my love," Michael interrupted. At that moment, she felt her possessed father standing behind her. He was holding a blanket and gently wrapped it around her shoulders.

"Sarah, you need to turn around and look at me," Michael whispered.

She slowly turned around to see her own father giving her a loving smile. It wasn't the kind of smile that a father would give his daughter. It was one that a man would give to his lover. Michael, staring at her like that through her father's eyes, felt disturbing to her. The entire situation was overwhelmingly surreal.

Sarah then looked at all the bodies lying on the floor. Were they dead? Had he killed them?

Please God! she thought. *Please say he didn't murder all of these people!*

"Are all these people dead?" she cried. Sarah then looked into his eyes and began to tremble. She felt warm tears running down her cheeks, and she was almost too afraid to hear the answer.

Michael looked at her as he gave her a loving and reassuring smile. He then took his hand and gently caressed her chin. With that, he placed a soft kiss upon her forehead.

"No, Sarah," he told her. "I promise you they're just asleep. They will all wake up in a few hours. By then, the two of us will have departed this realm. I know hurting people upsets you, Sarah. I don't want to upset you. Plus, there was no reason to kill them. There was no need for all these senseless deaths. Now, my dear, it's time we left. You wouldn't want to be late for your own wedding."

At this point, Sarah felt numb. She didn't say anything, nor did she react to him. Sarah knew there was nowhere for her to run. She was now his, and she didn't have any idea on how she could ever get away from him.

He then bent down and whispered in her ear, "I need you to go to sleep, Sarah." His voice was soothing and hypnotic. She immediately fell into a sleep-like trance as her body went limp in his arms.

***

Michael carefully scooped her up and cradled her lovingly. Again, he started to lean in for a passionate kiss.

"Could you please not do that in my brother's body?" asked Jonathan.

"You're right," said Michael. "I wasn't thinking. A parent should never act that way toward a child. I just know that it would bother Sarah. Besides, we need to leave soon anyway. I have a feeling that the local authorities are on their way."

Michael then noticed a stoic facial expression on Jonathan.

"Cheer up, Jonathan. Don't look so down all the time. It's not every day that one's daughter or even niece gets married. This should be a joyous occasion. I know I'm looking forward to it. Sarah, of course, will make the most beautiful bride."

"Just promise me you'll keep your word," said Jonathan.

"Don't worry, Jonathan," said Michael. "You will be rewarded, as you so rightfully deserve."

***

Chapter 21
Suite Memories

Eric and a squadron of police cars headed for the hospital.

When they arrived on the scene, hospital security was waiting for them.

"Lieutenant Johnson, you're not going to believe this," said a security guard.

"I don't know what to believe anymore, but try me," replied Eric.

"There is no access to the sixth floor," he told him. "The emergency exits are jammed, and none of the elevators will go to that floor. They just go right past it."

What the hell is going on? Eric wondered.

"Lieutenant!" called a hospital security guard as he made his way forward. "We were finally able to get the stairwell doors open!"

"All right," said Eric. "Let's find out what's going on. Move out!"

Eric led a brigade of determined police officers and hospital security. This included Officer Jenkins. Afraid of what might happen to Sarah, he practically raced up six flights of stairs. In his twenty-some years on the force, he had never had a case like this. Sarah was just so innocent. He had to protect her.

As he reached the sixth floor, he couldn't believe his eyes. The entire night staff was still lying unconscious. Eric then bent down and checked for a pulse on an unconscious nurse.

"Is she dead?" asked Officer Jenkins.

"No," replied Eric. "She's just unconscious. Check everyone on this floor, and try to find the girl. Look for her father and uncle as well. Is there any security footage?"

Ten police officers began searching the entire floor, but all they found were unconscious night staff and patients. There were no signs of Jonathan, Robert, or Sarah.

Eric felt like his head was about to explode. The search was coming up empty. Then, all of a sudden ...

"Lieutenant!" said another young officer. "We have the security footage, but we can't find the girl anywhere. Her father and uncle are also missing."

Eric shook his head. He wished they had more clues, but at least it was something.

"Well, at least let's check out the footage," said Eric.

He made his way into the room that contained the monitors for the sixth floor's cameras. As he watched the security footage, he saw Sarah faint into her father's arms. Jonathan was just standing there, while Robert scooped up his Sarah.

As Eric continued to watch the footage, he found a disturbing image.

"Officer," said Eric, "go back a little bit, and slow that last part down."

As the footage played again, Eric couldn't believe his eyes. It looked as though Robert was about to passionately kiss his unconscious daughter.

"That son of a bitch had me fooled!"

***

Michael sat in the backseat of Jonathan's car. He gently yet firmly held Sarah's unconscious body. He noticed that Jonathan kept staring back at him, through the rearview mirror.

"Keep your eyes on the road, Jonathan. I promise I will not do anything inappropriate in your brother's body."

Michael held his sleeping Sarah in his arms. Being corporeal brought back a lot of senses that were not as strong in his spirit form. As he lovingly cradled her, he breathed in the scent from her hair. She smelled even more delightful than he remembered. He ran Robert's fingers down her cheeks. Her skin was warm, soft, and delicate. With his eyes closed, he ran his fingers through her hair. More than anything, he wanted to kiss her, but he knew he shouldn't do that in her father's body.

"I've waited two hundred years for you, my love," he whispered. "Soon, my angel, we will be together forever. I promise I will always love you and bring you nothing but happiness. After we are married, we will fulfill each other's passionate desires. Nowadays, sixteen is still considered a child, but tonight, I shall make you a woman."

As he whispered, his hot breath warmed her neck. To his delight, he heard her let out a pleased sigh. Soon, she would be his—forever!

Jonathan drove them up to the manor. Gingerly, Michael lifted Sarah's unconscious body out of the car. He carried Sarah into the manor with Jonathan following them inside.

Michael headed toward the stairs with Sarah still in his arms. Jonathan stopped him before he went upstairs.

"Wait," said Jonathan. "Aren't you afraid the police will figure out we're here?"

"Even if they do," Michael sighed, "there is now a force-field surrounding the entire estate. They won't get through. The manor will be long gone before they even realize what's happening."

"But what'll happen to me?" asked Jonathan. "I'm still going to have a life to lead after all of this is over with. What if I end up in jail?"

"That's none of my concern," replied Michael. "My only concern is Sarah. Just like your only concern is Karen. Now, if you don't mind, I'm taking Sarah up to her bridal suite. After all, she has a wedding to prepare for. I'm sure she'll want to look as beautiful as she can for her husband-to-be."

Michael carried Sarah upstairs and then into the master bedroom. As he closed his eyes, the room changed. It was no longer dilapidated, like the rest of the manor. It was now an elegant master suite.

Michael gently laid Sarah upon the soft, comfortable bed. He then closed his eyes and concentrated on her physical injuries. Slowly, the bruises began to fade and her lip began to heal. Even the cracks in her ribs had successfully fused back together. He looked down upon her and smiled.

She again had the perfect angelic face that he loved. As she continued to rest, he gently stroked her delicate features. She would wake up soon but not yet. There were things he still needed to do for their wedding.

"Karen!" he called.

Karen's spirit soon appeared. She was amazed by what she saw. The room was now beautiful, unlike the rest of the rooms in the manor.

The suite itself was made up of a bedroom and a sitting room. The bedroom had a king-size four-point canopy bed. All the bedding and the settee were a rich burgundy color. Heavy burgundy velvet curtains hung in the windows.

Both rooms and the entire suite had hard cherrywood floors. The massive handcrafted ornate fireplace mantel was the focal point of the sitting room. The curtains and the sofas were also burgundy.

"How can this be?" she wondered aloud. She kept looking around the room.

Michael then saw Karen looking at him with an inquisitive look upon her face.

"Robert? Is that you?" she asked.

"Guess again, Karen," he responded.

"Michael? I mean, Lord Winworth, why are you in Robert's body?" she asked.

"Because your insignificant other kept failing me," he explained. "I had to take care of everything myself. This was the best way to get Sarah here."

"But why are you still in there?" she asked.

"Because I can read Robert's mind," he explained. "If I let him go, he will kill himself. He figures I can't use him as leverage if he's already dead. I would have Jonathan keep an eye on him, but Robert would likely end up dead."

"Jonathan's here?" she asked.

"Yes," he replied. "But that's not your concern right now. Your concern right now is Sarah. After she is well rested, you will help her get ready for the wedding."

"Oh my God!" Karen exclaimed. "Sarah! I didn't even see her." Karen then went straight toward her niece's side and knelt down beside her. She smiled at the sleeping girl and began to cry.

"I miss my loved ones so much," she cried.

"Well then," he sarcastically responded, "I guess this can be a nice bonding experience for you. Just make sure she's ready. After all, this is going to be the happiest day of her entire existence. This bedroom is only temporary. Soon, this suite and the rest of the manor will be permanently restored to its former glory. What do you think of it, my dear?"

"It's very lovely," replied Karen.

"Thank you, my dear," said Michael, "but the void can become much more than the manor itself. It will be able to transform into anything either Sarah or I wish. Sarah enjoyed the beach of the Amalfi Coast. I'm sure that she and I will visit it quite often."

"I'm sure she'll enjoy that," replied Karen sounding quite melancholy. Michael replied with a sarcastic chuckle.

"Thank you, Karen, not that I actually asked for your opinion about that," said Michael. "Now, if you will excuse me, I need to get to know my future father-in-law. Oh, by the way, the wedding's in two hours. I expect to see Sarah ready and at her most beautiful by then. You won't like what will happen to Todd if she's not." He then left the room.

***

Karen looked at Sarah sleeping peacefully. She had such a serene look upon her face. How was she going to feel about her upcoming nuptials? Why did it have to be too late to save her? Although she could never imagine how she could ever stop loving him, Karen was never going to forgive Jonathan for betraying their niece.

"Is that her?" a masculine voice asked.

Karen turned around and saw Jason with Todd. Their spirits must have entered the room without her noticing.

"Yes, that's her," Todd told him.

"Todd, Jason, what are you doing here?" she asked. "If Michael finds out—"

"I don't care, or give a damn about what Michael finds out about or doesn't find out about," said Jason. "I'm tired of his selfish and ruthless behavior toward others. He will kill to get what he wants. Even his love for this poor girl doesn't change anything. It doesn't matter what she wants. He will force her to marry him, and he will force her to do other things just to satisfy his own desires."

"Oh my God!" cried Karen. "Does Jonathan even realize what he's done?

"We just wanted to make sure she's okay," said Todd. "We're not going to stay long. As long as Michael is in Robert's body, he has no way of knowing we're here."

Todd then looked at Sarah.

"She is beautiful," Todd remarked. "You know, I had planned on looking her up five years from now, if we were both single. That's why Michael killed me. Now we will both be trapped here forever. I just hope he treats her the way she deserves to be treated."

"Yes, she does deserve a lot better than this," said Jason. "So, this is the angel who stole the demon's heart."

***

CHAPTER 22
The Lady of the Manor

As Michael walked around the manor, still inside Robert's body, he began to communicate with Robert.

"Well, what do you think of my humble abode?"

"It's a piece of shit!"

"I'll have you know that this is still one of the most massive estates in the United States—not only that but the entire world."

"Okay, it's a massive piece of shit!"

"You know, you really don't want to try my patience. I will not be disrespected in my home. Besides, we're going to be family soon."

"My daughter is not marrying you!"

"She will, or she will watch you die. I doubt she will choose the latter. I want Sarah to be happy. If you work with me, I will let you stay in the east wing. However, your time with her will be limited. It will be my choosing of when and for how long. I suggest you get on my good side."

"How thoughtful of Your Majesty. I'm just so honored that you'd even consider it."

"If that attitude doesn't change soon, you will soon regret it. True, I can't kill you. I need you alive so Sarah will agree to marry me. But you have no idea what I'm capable of, I can do far worse than just kill you."

"And what are you going to do to me? Take possession of my body? Kill my sister-in-law? Threaten her soul, so my brother obeys your every command? Kill Todd? Rape my daughter?"

"I did not rape Sarah! We made love!"

"Bullshit! I have your memories now! It was bad enough that you almost made me kiss her, but you molested her! You kept her from crying out for help!

I was in the next room, and I didn't even know she was being hurt! She was crying, and you kept her silent. I couldn't help her! Oh God! She was crying out for me, and you silenced her! I now have your memories of what you did to her! They are from your point of view!"

"I'm sorry I hurt her, but I stopped when I realized it!"

"Yes, but then you took control of her mind! You created some sort of little fantasy world! You manipulated her and used her own body to selfishly satisfy your own sick, twisted desires! Oh God! I can still see it unfold through your eyes. She tried to tell me, but I wouldn't listen!"

"I didn't do anything Sarah didn't want! That fantasy was hers! I gave in to her desires and let her choose what she wanted."

"You lowered her inhibitions. That's the same as drugging her. That is rape! Even if it had been completely, one hundred percent consensual, she is only sixteen. That automatically makes it rape!"

"Your laws don't apply here. This is my realm. Here, I make the laws, and here, I am God!"

"You can call yourself the emperor of dog shit, for all I care! But in the end, you know the truth! You're a rapist and a pedophile!"

Michael began to seethe with rage. Rapid, blood-pumping anger was building up inside. He didn't like being talked to in such a manner, but he knew he had to remain calm. If he harmed her father, Sarah would hate him. He then began to walk down to the cellar. As he kept walking, his anger slowly subsided.

"Let me show you some real rapists."

Michael could sense that Robert was doing all he could to avoid seeing the torturous display that was unfolding right before them.

"That one there, he is getting the worst of it. That was Alex. I wouldn't pity him if I were you. He's the one who put filth in your daughter's mouth! Look at him!"

"No, I refuse to look at your twisted and depraved sense of justice!"

"Look at him!"

"No!"

"I said look at him! Do not feel empathy or any kind of sorrow for him! He was violently raping your daughter! I read his mind. I read all their minds! They were planning on killing her and then throwing her away like common garbage!"

121

Remembering how much he hated these three men, Robert allowed himself to see what was happening to their captured souls. Two of them were completely and constantly engulfed in flames. One of them, Alex, had his entire ghostly form constantly being eaten alive by fire ants.

"Oh my God! I'm her own her father! Even I wouldn't wish this on them!"

"If she hadn't cried out for help—*my* help—she would be dead right now! I was there to save her life, *not* you! You were the one who left her alone! If anything, you should be grateful! You should be enjoying the torturous hell that I am personally bestowing upon them!"

"My daughter would be horrified by this! Any rational, thinking human being would be horrified by what you are doing to them! She will never love one as evil and barbaric as you! You're a sadistic, murdering son of a bitch!"

"Oh? As I recall, you told Lieutenant Johnson that you hoped they'd never find me, that I was a hero, not a murderer."

"How did you know that I said that?"

"Because I wanted to make sure my angel was okay. So my spirit went to the hospital to keep an eye on her. I went to her right after I paid your worthless brother Jonathan a visit."

"Jonathan is no longer my brother, all thanks to you! You have destroyed my family! I will never, under any circumstances, let you marry my daughter!"

"You don't have a say in the matter!"

"You say you love Sarah, but eternity is a long time to spend with a person. What happens when one day she isn't doing all that you want her to? How will you punish her then? Like these three men? Or maybe you'll violently rape her? As your own mother did to you?"

"Shut up! My mother loved me!"

"Apparently."

This only angered Michael further.

"Believe me, you are going to pay for this! I haven't figured out how yet, but you will! And I will never, under any circumstances, punish or harm my Sarah! I love her, and soon she will love me!"

"Go to hell!"

Michael laughed maniacally.

"You know, I can't wait until our wedding night when I take her sweet virginity. Since it'll be her first time, she'll be nice and tight. Touching her soft, young, naked, and nubile flesh. She will be begging me for more, and I will gladly give it to her. She will scream my name in ecstasy, and I will scream her name as well. We will experience pleasures you can't even comprehend! Well, at least pleasures that poor Helen never got to experience."

"You son of a bitch! Don't you dare talk about my wife! And don't even think about touching my daughter! Or I swear I'll—"

"Or you'll what? You know what? I'm sick of you! I think I'll I just silence you for a while. I won't hear from you until the wedding. Don't worry. I'll let you give the bride away.

***

Sarah began to wake up from her sleep. She had no idea where she was. Wherever it was, the room was amazing. She then let out a scream, as she noticed three ghostly apparitions staring at her.

"Sarah, Sarah, it's okay," said the female one. "You're okay."

Sarah began to relax a little. It took her a while, but she eventually recognized two of the spirits right in front of her. One was dressed like a maid, the other like a gardener. They looked the same. But their spirited apparitions were a bluish color, while their eyes were dark and lifeless.

"Aunt Karen?" she asked. "Todd?"

"Yes, sweetie, we're here," replied Karen.

She and Sarah shared a loving embrace.

"You're so cold," said Sarah. She then looked at Todd and began to cry. "Todd! I'm sorry! It's my fault you're here!"

"No, Sarah, it's not," replied Todd reassuringly. "Like I told you before, you can't blame yourself for everything. Life happens sometimes, as well as death."

"He's right," said the other man.

"I'm sorry," Sarah replied. "I don't think I know you."

"You wouldn't," Karen replied. "I'm sorry, let me introduce you. Jason, this is Sarah. Sarah, this is Jason Winworth."

He smiled at her, gently took her hand, and kissed the back of it. Both his hands and his lips were ice cold."

"It's a pleasure to make your acquaintance, my lady," he told her. "I just wish it were under different circumstances."

"You're his brother," said Sarah. "You're the one he used to create all of this."

"And you are the angel who enchanted the demon," he responded. "You are a very lovely young woman. I can see why he loves you so much. Of course, he always did prefer lovely young women, but there's something different about you. He sees it, as I do." He then smiled and winked at her.

Sarah smiled back, and she blushed. Even as a spirit, Sarah could tell he was a handsome and charming man.

"A-hem!"

Michael had just entered the room, carrying a huge metal lockbox. He was still possessing Robert's body. He cleared his throat to let his presence be known and then set the box down on the settee in front of the bed.

"I hope you aren't getting any ideas, Brother!" said Michael.

"Of course not, Michael," Jason replied. "I was just getting to know my future sister-in-law."

"As long as you realize that's all she'll be to you," said Michael. "Why are you and Todd in here anyway? You're interrupting female bonding time."

"I'm sorry, Lord Winworth. We were just—" Todd began.

"I didn't ask you!" exclaimed Michael. "I asked Jason!"

"Before Todd was so rudely interrupted," Jason began, "we were checking up on her well-being, Michael."

"You're trying my patience, Jason!" Michael responded.

Jason just glared at him in defiance.

"Are you going to punish me, Michael?" asked Jason. "Do you really want your future wife to see that?"

Michael then looked over at Sarah. He didn't like seeing the terror in her eyes, especially since it was because of him.

"I think it would be best, Jason," said Michael in a much calmer tone, "if you and Todd left right now. Karen, I need some alone time with Sarah. I will call you when I'm done. Then you can help her get ready. Why don't you go find Jonathan? I'm sure he'd love to talk to you. My guess is that you have a few choice words of your own, just for him."

With that, the three spirits disappeared. He looked at Sarah and smiled.

"Come here, my dear. I have my wedding presents for you," he told her.

"I-I didn't get you anything," she responded.

He just smiled at her.

"Your being here is the only the present I need," he told her.

"Th-thank you, Lord Winworth," she said.

Michael furrowed his brow.

"Sarah," he began, "there is no need to call me that. You can call me Michael or any other little pet name you want for me. I have the same option with you. That's why I call you my angel. You will be the lady of the manor. They will only refer to you as Lady Winworth, just as they are to refer to me as Lord Winworth."

Sarah was even more confused.

"Why?" she asked. "Why do they even have to be servants? You'll have me. Can't you just let them all go?"

"All estates need good servants," he said. "Besides, they brought this on themselves. Most of them tried to destroy me. Then Todd, Alex, and those other two, they tried to take what was mine."

"Why do you have to be so cruel to them?" she asked. "Haven't they all suffered enough?"

He just smiled at her but ignored her question. He then unlocked the box and showed her what was inside.

***

"Look what I have for you, my love," he said. He opened it and revealed over a million dollars' worth of jewelry. Michael was amused by the wide-eyed look of astonishment upon her face. He grabbed a tiara from inside. It was the one she had worn to the ball.

"You probably thought that I made up the jewelry," he said. "True, I had to imagine it, when we were inside your unconscious mind. But what I imagined really does exist. This jewelry has been in my family for generations. There is much more than what's in here. This is just a sample. It's all yours, my dear. I can't think of anyone more worthy of it than you.

Sarah sweetly smiled at him, though she was obviously nervous. He couldn't help but find her naïveté quite charming. Michael put the tiara back in the box. He then took out another tiara; this one was made of all diamonds. He kept smiling, as he placed it on her head.

"I would like for you to wear this," he told her. "I want to see a beautiful queen, my beautiful queen, walking down the aisle toward her loving husband-to-be."

"Thank you, Michael," she replied. She looked at him and gave him a nervous smile. Then she quickly looked away.

"I have a beautiful diamond necklace for you to wear as well," said Michael. "You'll just have to remove the locket for the ceremony."

He went to reach both hands behind her neck, so that he could remove the locket. With a wide look of fear in her eyes, she grabbed the locket.

"No!" she cried, "Please don't! You know how important it is to me!" She then backed away before his hands reached the clasp.

Michael noticed the concerned look on her face and smiled at her.

"I promise it would only be for the ceremony," he told her.

Tears began to well up in her eyes, and she began shaking her head.

"No!" she cried. "I can't. I won't. I promised my father and myself that I will never take it off. I will always wear it close to my heart. As long as I wear it, I can never forget how much he loves me."

As she looked up at him with tears in her beautiful green eyes, he knew he couldn't deny her. Her outer beauty was undeniable, but her inner beauty, her very soul, was truly a rare treasure to behold. He looked at her and smiled. He took his right hand and gently cupped her chin.

"How could I say no that beautiful face of yours," he told her. "You are such a rare beauty. I bet you don't realize it, do you? You're like an enchantress, but you don't even know it."

Sarah began to blush as a shy smile escaped her lips. He couldn't help but smile at her pure innocence.

"You know," he began, "a woman as lovely as you does deserve the finest of jewelry. But a goddess doesn't really need to wear that much. Perhaps the tiara and the diamond necklace would be a bit too much. Your smile is pure perfection, my dear. If wearing the locket makes you happy, then who am I to stand in the way of pure perfection? Of course you may wear the locket."

"Thank you," she said. She then gave him a genuine smile. At that moment, she looked so beautiful, she could have melted even the darkest of hearts. She had already melted this demon's heart.

Michael then put the necklace back in the box.

"Now, I believe it's time we made this official," said Michael. He pulled out a small velvet box. With a loving smile, he got down on one knee. He then opened it, revealing the beautiful, nearly flawless five-carat diamond ring. He could tell by the astonished look upon her face that it was probably the biggest diamond Sarah had ever seen. He chuckled in amusement over her innocence and almost childlike wonder. Michael then placed the ring upon her finger.

"Sarah Gilmore, will you marry me?"

***

CHAPTER 23
Familial Bonds

Jonathan was sitting on the steps in the foyer, riddled with guilt. He kept staring at the floor. *How did things get to this point?* Jonathan couldn't help but notice the irony of his surroundings. Just like his life, this once glorious manor was now broken and crumbling around him. He wondered if there was a point to anything anymore.

"Jon," he heard a sweet familiar voice say.

There she was, the love of his life. But she was now an unfortunate spirit, trapped inside a decaying prison. The optimism that had made her shine was now gone. She was a displaced soul. He was saddened to see her forced to wear a chambermaid's uniform.

"Karen!" he cried. "Oh my God! What has he done to you?" He then went to her and embraced her cold, ghostly form. Jonathan began to cry. The chill was just a reminder of what he had lost. She was always so heartwarming, but she was literally a chilling reminder of her former self.

"Why, Jonathan?" she asked. "Why did you do it? How could you do this to Robert? How could you do this to Sarah?"

"I didn't have a choice, Karen," cried Robert. "I couldn't stand the thought of you trapped here forever. I would do anything for you. I love you. It's not like he will mistreat Sarah. He loves her. If anything, he'd worship her, just like I should be doing with you."

"A gilded cage is still a prison, Jonathan," cried Karen. "We never had children of our own. Sarah was the closest we ever had to a daughter. You shouldn't have betrayed her like that. I will always love you, Jonathan. But I don't know if I can forgive you."

"Karen," replied Jonathan, "he threatened you, and Todd, if I didn't help him. I couldn't let him hurt you."

"I know," she replied. "But you let it get that far. You should have ignored Lord Winworth's first warning. You should have told Robert the truth."

"Lord Winworth?" asked Jonathan. "That son of a bitch is making you call him Lord Winworth?"

"Please, Jonathan, not so loud," said Karen. "I don't want him to be angry with you."

"Believe me, Karen, Lord Winworth is plenty angry with me," he said in snarky tone. "I've pissed him off plenty of times. But as long as he's in Robert's body, he is somewhat limited in what he can hear. I'm glad know that at least you still care about me."

"I will always love and care for you, Jonathan," Karen said and smiled. "Even when you make mistakes, which is a lot."

Jonathan just smiled back at her.

"Karen, listen to me," he began. "I didn't come here without some knowledge of the situation. I found Father Thomas's notes in a vault at city hall."

"What were his notes doing at city hall?" she asked.

"Apparently, they were discovered a little more than a century after that infamous night," Jonathan replied. "Whoever was in charge at the time decided to lock it up in the vault."

"What are you saying, Jonathan?" asked Karen.

"I'm saying I've been reading some of Father Thomas's notes," Jonathan told her, "the ones he took while studying the kind of dark magic Michael was using. It turns out that whoever's the life-force controls the void. That means Sarah, not Michael, will be in charge. She can expel him and then release all the souls."

"But then she'll be trapped here forever, alone," replied Karen.

"She wouldn't have to be," said Jonathan. "We could stay here. We would be together forever. So could Robert and Todd. The five of us would be a family."

"Jonathan," replied Karen, "don't you see? That's no better than what Lord Winworth is trying."

"Lord Winworth, Lord Winworth!" he exclaimed. "I'm sick of hearing about Lord Winworth. I know it isn't the best solution, but it's better than what he has planned. As soon as they're married, we'll inform her. Sarah will do the right thing. She will help everyone. She'll be the one with the power."

"Do you really think my brother hasn't thought of this already?" asked Jason as his spirit manifested itself before them. "I assure you he has already figured out a way around it. He always does."

"Who are you?" asked Jonathan.

"Jonathan, this is Jason, Jason Winworth," Karen replied. "Jason, this is Jonathan, Jonathan Gilmore, my husband."

"You're a lucky man," said Jason. "Karen as made my existence a little easier around here."

"What the hell is that supposed to mean?" asked Jonathan.

"Jonathan!" exclaimed Karen. "It's not like that. Unfortunately, our situation has forced us all to support one another. You are the only man I love. Besides, what you're hinting is impossible."

"You're right," said Jonathan. "I'm sorry. It's just that these last two months have been hell without you, Karen."

"It's been hard on me too," replied Karen. "I shouldn't be so quick to judge. If it was your soul that had been taken, I might have made a similar bargain with Lord Winworth."

"I'm sorry too, Jason," said Jonathan. "I shouldn't have jumped to conclusions. I need to remember that you are not your brother."

"It's okay," said Jason. "I understand."

"Are you sure that Michael knows the truth about the life-force being the true power?" asked Jonathan.

"No," replied Jason, "but I know my brother. He probably does know, and he's probably already figured out a loophole."

***

"Sarah Gilmore, will you marry me?" asked Michael, who was still in Robert's body.

She had dreamed of this moment most of her life but not with her father popping the question.

"I-I—" she began.

Just then his entire body started to tremble, and his eyes tightly closed shut.

"S-sarah, n-*no!*" cried Robert.

His body continued shaking, and his eyes remained tightly shut. There was an apparent inner struggle.

"Daddy?" cried Sarah.

Then, all of a sudden, her father's body stopped shaking, and he opened his eyes.

"Well, I'll give your father credit," said Michael. "He is strong willed."

"Please let me talk to him!" she cried.

"I'll will do better than that," he told her. "Say yes, and I will leave his body. Say no, and he dies like Todd. You know this is inevitable, Sarah. Don't try to make it harder than it needs to be."

Tears formed in Sarah's eyes as she looked up at him.

"All right," she replied. "I will marry you."

He looked at her and smiled. Then, with a loud gasp, Michael's spirit began to flow from out of her father's eyes. Robert was now free, but his obviously weakened body fell to the floor. Sarah immediately went to help her father.

"Daddy!" she cried, as she began to embrace him.

"He will be weak for a bit, but he'll be fine," said Michael.

Sarah looked up and was surprised to see Michael's ghostly form hovering over them. Before, she had only seen him in her dreams, where he had been corporeal.

"Sarah!" cried Robert, as he returned her embrace. "Sarah, please don't worry about me. Don't marry him. He's evil!"

"She has already agreed," said Michael. "If she changes her mind, I will not only kill you; I will kill Jonathan. Please, Sarah, I love you. Don't make me do things I don't want to do."

"You're a damn liar and a sadist!" exclaimed Robert. "Why don't you show her how much you really love her? Why not show her the cellar?"

"What's in the cellar?" asked Sarah.

"Let's just say that Alex and his friends are getting what they deserve," replied Michael. "As I said before, no one hurts my angel and gets away with it."

"Show me!" demanded Sarah with tears forming in her eyes. "I want to see it!"

"Very well," said Michael. "But just keep in mind what they did to you and what they were going to do to you."

Michael opened his hand, and a glowing orb soon appeared. A view from the cellar was now visible. Sarah screamed when she saw the three hapless victims. Realizing that it was too much for her, Michael immediately cut the visual link between her and the cellar. But the horrific image would be forever ingrained within her mind.

Sarah was crying and buried her face in her father's shoulder. The image in the vision was horrible. All three of were there, screaming in agony and begging for mercy. She couldn't stand to see them suffer like that, no matter what they had done to her. She felt responsible. She was the one who had called for Michael's help.

"Why did you bring them here?" she cried. "Why not let God decide their fate?"

"Where do you think they would have ended up, Sarah?" asked Michael. "Do you believe hell would have been easier on them?"

"No!" she cried. "But I wouldn't be married to Satan. I wouldn't be part of any of it."

"I don't know, Sarah," said Robert with a smug look upon his face. "He seems pretty close to Satan to me."

Robert and Michael just stared at one another. Both of them had angry, stoic looks upon their faces.

"Sarah," said Michael, "I hope this isn't changing your mind."

"No," said Sarah, "I agreed to marry you. I will keep my promise."

"Sarah, don't!" cried Robert.

"Daddy, please!" she cried. "I don't want any more people trapped here, especially you!"

"That's my good girl," said Michael, smiling at her. He then waved his hand and forced Robert off the floor. Robert was thrown into a sitting position and pinned against the wall. A force field enveloped him and held him against the wall.

"Daddy!" cried Sarah.

"He's all right, Sarah," said Michael. "I don't have any other choice. Remember, we shared a mind for a couple of hours. If I don't keep him like this, he'll kill himself. He figures that if he's already dead, I can't get you to agree to our upcoming nuptials. Keep in mind, my love. I always have a few backup plans."

"You don't have to hurt him!" she cried. "I said I would marry you!"

"Good," Michael replied. "Because I don't want to hurt him. In fact, after we're married, I'm going to allow him to live in the entire east wing. The times you two will spend together will be few and far between, and the amount of time will be limited as well. But you will be able to see one another, once in a while." He looked at her and smiled.

"Thank you," she said, returning the smile.

"Now, I will call for Karen," he said. "But before I do ..." He grabbed her and kissed her passionately. Even though his embrace and lips were ice cold, she didn't resist. She still yearned for him and returned his passion. Again, there was no manipulation on his part. Robert kept struggling to break free. But the force field just held him in place.

"Karen!" cried Michael.

She appeared.

"Yes, Lord Winworth," Karen replied. "Robert?"

"Never mind that!" Michael snarled. "You are here to help the future Lady Winworth prepare for our wedding, not to socialize with the father of the bride. Keep in mind, Karen, you now only have an hour and a half. There's a wedding dress and a veil for Sarah in the bedroom, as well as a tiara. Take her into the bedroom, and help her get ready."

"Yes, Lord Winworth," replied Karen.

"You bastard!" screamed Robert.

Michael walked right up to Robert and smiled.

"No," said Michael, "I'm afraid you have it backward. My brother Jason is the bastard. I'm the son of a bitch."

***

Chapter 24
Prewedding Jitters

Back at the police station, Eric was trying to figure out where Sarah was. He had never felt so perplexed by any other case before this one, even after serving twenty years on the police force.

The police checked every inch of the hospital. Robert, Jonathan, and Sarah were nowhere to be found. The only clues they had were the hospital security footage. But then one thing kept burning in the back of his mind—Mimi telling him that she had overheard Robert say that he had come to take Sarah home.

Home? He came to take her home, thought Eric. *Are both her father and her uncle delusional? Do they both think they're Michael Winworth? If so, why would they take her all the way back to Robert's house if—Oh my God! If they both believe they're Michael Winworth, then home wouldn't be Robert's house. Home would be the manor. That's where she is. They took her to the manor!*

***

Michael was down in the cellar looking at what he called his masterpiece. The three men who had attacked Sarah were being continuously tortured. Michael reveled in their pain. They had hurt the only person for whom he had ever really given a damn.

"Please stop!" cried Alex.

They had never before even imagined such pain could exist.

"Now why would I want to do that?" asked Michael. "I'm having so much fun. You see, you not only mentally and physically abused my angel; you degraded her! Believe me, I'm just getting started. I can't wait until you three become corporeal, then I'm really going to have some fun. You know I've always wanted to see someone be drawn, and quartered."

Alex and the others continued to scream in pain. Michael laughed manically, as he took great delight in their suffering.

"You know, I never understand," said Michael, "why a man would have to beat a woman just to get her into his bed. I, of course, never had to do that. I could always get any woman I wanted. I've probably even fathered a few bastards around Europe. Then again, I had charm, wealth, intelligence, and, of course, my devilishly good looks. You know, four qualities that you gentlemen don't seem to possess."

"Please!" cried Alex. "Stop! Stop the horrendous pain! I'll do anything you ask!"

"Anything?" asked Michael. "Fine! I want you to beg. I want you to beg, like you made Sarah beg! And I want you to beg like all your other victims did as well!"

"All right!" cried Alex. "I'm sorry! I'm sorry I hurt them. I'm sorry for the mental and physical anguish I have caused, especially her. But, please, stop this pain! Have mercy! I can't take it anymore. Please help me!"

"There now, see?" said Michael. "That wasn't so difficult, was it? Now if you gentlemen will excuse me, I'm getting married soon. I need to get ready."

"Wait!" screamed Alex. "You said if I begged, you would stop the torture!"

Michael just looked at him with a wicked smile.

"No, I'm afraid you misunderstood," replied Michael. "See, you said you would do whatever I wanted, and you did. I never said that if you did, I would stop it. But I do want to thank you. After all, I am getting married. It's nice to have some amusement, to ease my anxiety. And I have found all of this rather … amusing. Now, it is getting late. You three are not invited. So, I'm afraid I have to bid you gentlemen adieu." He then turned his back on them as they continued to scream in pain and just walked away.

***

Robert was still trapped against the wall. He kept trying and struggling to get out of the force field, but it was no use. Just then, Jonathan entered the room. Robert glared at him in rage.

"Robert," Jonathan began, "I—"

"Get the fuck away from me, Jonathan," Robert growled. "You sold my daughter to a rapist!"

"I had no choice, Robert," said Jonathan. "He said if I didn't find him a bride, Karen would be trapped here forever."

"So you decided to give him Sarah?" asked a disgusted Robert.

"No," replied Jonathan, "I didn't know that Sarah had changed so much. If I had, I would have told you not to bring her. But as soon as he saw her, he wanted her. It was never my intention to give him Sarah, but he insisted. I tried to get him to reconsider, but he fell in love with her. He was going to have her no matter what."

"Wait!" said Robert. "Is this why you stole money from the city treasury? You were going to trap some other defenseless girl from the college? That's the reason you told me to take Sarah away from here, isn't it? But you changed your mind. You also tried to convince me that Todd was a womanizer. You're a piece of shit! Why couldn't you just tell me the truth?"

"Would you have even believed me?" asked Jonathan. "Besides, it wouldn't have mattered. He already saw Sarah. He was going to have her no matter what. I couldn't have stopped him if I tried. I never wanted to hurt Sarah or you. You're my brother. I—"

"Don't say it, Jonathan!" exclaimed Robert. "You're dead to me! I have no brother!"

"Robert, I'm sorry! I don't know what else to say," Jonathan pleaded.

He didn't even respond and acted as if Jonathan were no longer there. Robert stared at the closed door to the bedroom. His little girl was getting ready for a wedding to an evil beast. And there wasn't a damn thing he could do about it.

***

Sarah was getting ready for the wedding. Somehow, Michael had turned the master suite's water closet into a fully functioning modern-day bathroom. Sarah was relieved that she could get a hot shower. When she finished drying her hair, Karen started to help her get ready.

"I know brides wear their hair up these days," said Karen. "But you've always had such beautiful hair. I think you should wear it down."

Sarah looked at herself in the mirror. It was then that she realized her injuries had been healed. Michael had even removed the pain from her abdomen. He must have healed her cracked ribs as well.

"Aunt Karen," cried Sarah, "I'm too young for this! I'm only sixteen, and he died when he was thirty-five. Even if he wasn't so much older than me, I'm too young to get married. Oh, Aunt Karen, what am I going to do?"

Sarah couldn't stop crying. She had always thought her wedding day would be the happiest of her life.

Sarah then felt her aunt's ghostly form embrace her lovingly.

"I wish I had the answer, sweetheart, but I don't," her aunt replied.

Sarah reciprocated her aunt's embrace. Then she remembered that Michael had demanded that they be on time. Not wanting others to suffer and knowing she wasn't ready, Sarah started to compose herself.

"I guess I need to get ready," said Sarah.

Karen looked at Sarah and smiled. She helped her with her hair and makeup. It was sad. Sarah used to imagine doing this with her own mother. However, she knew her mother would never want to be a part of this.

Karen then took the dress out of the closet and brought it over to Sarah.

"That's a beautiful gown!" exclaimed Karen. "I wonder why he chose it."

"He's been in my mind," replied Sarah. "A couple of years ago, Mom and I went to get our hair done. While we were waiting, I flipped through a bridal magazine. I was in awe of this dress. It's the one I thought would someday be perfect for me. The way I feel now, it doesn't seem so perfect anymore."

After Karen helped her into the dress and then placed the veil in the back of her hair, she looked at Sarah and began to cry.

"Sarah, you look beautiful!" cried Karen. "I guess we should show your father."

With that, they opened the door to the sitting area. When she entered the room, her father just stared at her.

"My God, Sarah!" exclaimed a teary-eyed Robert. "You're beautiful!"

***

CHAPTER 25
An Unholy Matrimony

Robert was in complete awe of his daughter. He had never seen her look more beautiful. There she stood in a long white ball gown. The entire gown was covered in mesh lace and crystals. The long sleeves were only mesh lace and off the shoulder. To top it all off, she wore a diamond tiara and a long mesh veil. But, best of all, she was still wearing the locket.

Tears came to his eyes. And for a split second, he wished Helen was there to see her. But then he remembered whom Sarah was marrying and why.

"You look amazing!" said Jonathan.

"Thank you, Uncle Jon," replied Sarah, and she smiled.

"Let's cut the bullshit!" cried Robert. "This is not a happy occasion. My daughter's about to marry the devil himself, and you're all acting like this is okay!"

"No, Robert," said Karen, "we're not. We're just trying to make the best of a bad situation. If you can think of a way out of this, I'm all ears. I don't want Sarah to have to marry Lord Winworth either."

"Lord Winworth?" asked Robert. "Karen, do you even hear yourself? This madman has everyone so twisted and afraid. I mean, I'm just supposed to let my daughter marry this evil megalomaniac?"

"Then come up with an alternative solution, Robert!" demanded Jonathan.

"Go to hell, Jonathan!" spat Robert.

"Please stop!" cried Sarah. "I can't take anymore. Does anyone even care how I feel? This is all my fault. If it weren't for me, our family wouldn't be tearing apart!"

"It's not your fault, Sarah," said Karen. "If you want to play that game, you can say it's my fault. I'm the one who tried to have this place torn down. If I hadn't, I'd still be alive. Your father wouldn't have been involved, and Lord Winworth wouldn't even know you exist. Todd would also still be alive. If anyone is to blame, it's me."

"Karen," Jonathan cried, "I'm the one to blame. I got the ball rolling on the demolition plans for this place. I mean, if any—"

"Oh, it's everybody's fault! It's nobody's fault!" cried Robert. "I really don't give a shit! It's not going to change the fact that my daughter is about to marry a monster!"

"Daddy!" cried Sarah.

Robert looked over at his daughter. His heart was breaking, as he could see tears in her eyes. He could tell by the way she was looking at him that she was pleading with him to understand. But he just couldn't.

"I'm sorry, sweetheart," cried Robert. "I just love you so much. I dreamt of this day, or rather dreaded this day, since I first held you in my arms. I wanted so much for you. Now you're going to be imprisoned by some pervert for all eternity."

"At least he loves me, Daddy," said Sarah.

"Sarah, you're only sixteen," said Robert. "You don't even know what that kind of love is. You should be waiting at least five years before you would even consider getting married. And it should be with someone who has nothing but pure, unconditional love. But this man's love is dark and possessive. He had a messed-up childhood. I have some of his memories. His twisted love for you may be the only way he knows how to love."

"So you know about my brother's dark past?" said Jason.

Robert turned around. He saw Todd's and a younger man's spirits manifest themselves.

"Who the hell are you?" asked Robert.

"I'm Jason Winworth, Michael's brother," replied Jason. "I'm not an admirer of my brother's either," said Jason. "He forever separated me from my wife. I hate him."

"Well, Jason, I'm sorry for your situation," Robert began, "but unless you have a solution, I really don't give a damn."

"I don't want him getting what he wants. He doesn't deserve it," Jason replied. "He sure as hell doesn't deserve your daughter."

"Then come up with an alternative!" Robert demanded. "If you're his brother, then you know him better than anyone!"

"You're right. I do know him better than anyone," said Jason. "I'm sorry, but there is no alternative. Even if Sarah chooses your dying over her marrying him, he will find another way. If I know my brother, he will kill everyone in this town, one by one, until she does say yes."

"Can't you think of any way to sneak her out of here?" asked Robert.

"There is a force field around this estate, as well as this house," Jason replied. "No one can get in or out. She can't escape. He will never let her go. I've never seen him care about anyone else besides himself—not until Sarah came into his existence. But you are right; his love is possessive. He is willing to put her needs before his—except for one, his need to have her."

"So then tell me, Mr. Winworth," cried Robert, "what in the hell am I supposed to do?"

"If there was something you could do, I would be the first to help you," said Jason, "but there isn't any way to stop this wedding. I'm sorry. Just be thankful he's letting you stay. But be warned—if you do stay, don't cross him. Except for Sarah, anyone else who crosses him will suffer dire consequences."

Robert hung his head and began to cry. They were right. There was no way to stop it. Sarah walked over to her father, lifted his head up, and smiled.

"Daddy, please don't make this any harder than it has to be," she pleaded.

"Oh, Sarah, my beautiful baby girl," cried Robert. "I'm sorry I didn't protect you, and I'm sorry I didn't believe you. I've failed you as a father. Despite that, please never forget how much I love you."

Sarah looked down at the locket and lifted it up a little to show him.

"As long as I have this," Sarah said, crying, "I will always remember just how much you really do love me." She smiled and then gave him a peck on the cheek.

Todd walked over to Sarah and smiled.

"I just wanted to tell you how beautiful you look," said Todd.

She smiled back at him.

"Ten years ago, I used to dream of this moment," she said. "Me standing next to you while I'm wearing a wedding dress. I'm sorry that I was only able to express myself by kicking you."

"That's okay," said Todd. "That's the only way six-year-olds know how to express their feelings for those they like. It might have been a nice wedding."

Sarah smiled, and a few tears ran down her face.

"Thank you," she replied.

"Maybe you can show your affection toward Lord Winworth by kicking him," said a smug Robert.

Jason then looked up toward the ceiling.

"He's calling us. I'm afraid it's time."

***

Lieutenant Eric Johnson led a cavalcade of squad cars. They had just left the police station and were racing toward the manor. *What the hell were they planning on doing with her?*

The possibilities frightened him. He cared about all the victims he had ever helped, but Sarah was different. She was just like his Erica. Both were full of life and empathetic toward others. He was afraid that if he couldn't save her, he would be letting Erica down as well.

If Sarah could easily fall victim to those who would seek to take advantage of her, then so could Erica. True, Erica was older but only by a couple of years. It was those who cared about others the most who usually got hurt.

Eric was driving with Officer Jenkins, who sat in the passenger seat. They were coming up on the manor when, all of a sudden, *bam!* The car crashed into something. Fortunately, the airbags deployed. *What the hell happened?* He then looked over at Officer Jenkins.

"Carolyn?" he asked. "Are you all right?"

"I'm okay," she moaned. "What did we just hit?"

They both got out of the car. Eric walked to the front of the car. It had hit something, but there was nothing there. He then placed his hand on the invisible barrier. To his confusion, it felt solid. As he kept his hand on the barrier, multicolored electrical charges were drawn to it. The rest of the squadron had stopped once they saw the lieutenant's car hit the force field.

"Lieutenant," asked another officer, "are you all right? What happened?"

Eric just stared at the electrical charges.

"I have no idea," he replied. He then took out his gun and fired at the invisible barrier. To his surprise, the bullet bounced right off of it.

What the hell is going on?

***

Karen, Todd, and Jason had been summoned to the grand ballroom. The three of them stood up at the altar with Michael, while the other trapped souls stood on either side of the aisle. All of them were dressed up as servants, in nineteenth-century-style uniforms.

Michael closed his eyes and restored the ballroom, making it look the same as it once had. It looked like the one Michael had created in Sarah's mind for their first meeting. There was an orchestra. They weren't even ghosts, just some apparitions that Michael had made up in his head.

"Just like the bridal suite, this ballroom is temporary—for now, but not for long," said Michael. "Now, I suppose it's time I get ready."

The ghostly outfit he had been wearing all of a sudden changed. Instead of nineteenth-century attire, he decided to dress in a more modern fashion. After all, Sarah would. He chose an expensive-looking tuxedo. He wanted to look his best for Sarah.

"Well, my dear brother, aren't you going to comment on how I look?" asked Michael. "After all, this is the most important day of my existence."

"Do you really want my opinion?" asked Jason in a snide manner.

"No," said Michael, "probably not. What do you think, Karen?"

"You look handsome as always," she replied.

"Thank you, my dear," he said and smiled. "You know, I did consider you at one time, even though you were already married—but then again, so was Pauline. I'm afraid that you and I just didn't have the same connection that I have with my Sarah."

"Yes, lucky her," replied Karen in a snarky tone.

"Do not disrespect, Karen," growled Michael.

"P-please," Karen begged, "forgive me, Lord Winworth."

"Lucky for you, my dear," said Michael, "or rather for your dear brother and mine, I'm willing to look over this little indiscretion. After all, it is my wedding day. It's a day of love and celebration. Just don't let it happen again!"

"Y-yes, yes, Lord Winworth. Th-thank you," replied Karen, as a look of fear spread across her ghostly face.

"Why are we standing up here anyway, Michael?" asked Jason.

"Karen is up here as Sarah's matron of honor," replied Michael. "Just as you are my best man. I thought I should return the favor. After all, I served as best man at your wedding."

"Don't remind me," Jason growled.

***

Jonathan, Robert, and Sarah were still in the master suite. Then, all of a sudden, Robert noticed that the force field had disappeared around him. This was it; his daughter's fate was sealed. How could he hand his little girl over to the madman?

"I guess it's time for us to go," said Jonathan.

"So help me, Jonathan," cried Robert, "if you just say one more word to me, your head will hit the floor."

"Daddy, please! This is difficult enough as it is," cried Sarah.

"Fine," replied Robert. More than anything, he wanted to grab Sarah and get the hell out of there. But he knew it would be pointless. He had heard police sirens, so he knew Eric had figured out where they were. But he also knew that the police would be no match for Michael. Even if they were, they'd never get through the force field.

As they left the master suite, the magnificent room again became dilapidated. The furniture disappeared, the hardwood floors became warped, and the heavy curtains were replaced by cobwebs. What had been a warm and relaxed atmosphere now seemed cold and empty.

Robert walked down the stairs with his arm around his daughter. Jonathan was following behind. With each step that he took to go down the stairs, he became angrier. Robert's jaw clenched, and his heart began to race.

As they reached the ground floor, a ghostly apparition of a man appeared. He was dressed like a nineteenth-century butler. Like the other spirits, he was transparent and was bluish in color. Robert just stared into the spirit's cold, dead eyes.

"This way," the spirit informed them, and they followed him to the grand ballroom.

***

Michael stood at the altar, waiting for his angel to arrive. When Sarah appeared with her father and uncle at the entrance to the ballroom, Michael couldn't believe what he was seeing. He didn't think it was possible, but Sarah was even more beautiful than he could have ever imagined.

Just then, the orchestra started to play "Canon in D," and Robert walked Sarah down the aisle, while Jonathan walked close behind them.

As Sarah made her way toward Michael, he couldn't help but smile. His beloved angel would soon be his. He was going to love her and grant her every heart's desire. And she would love him in return.

"You look exquisite, my love," said Michael as she reached the altar. "I cannot wait until after the ceremony."

Sarah's eyes became wide, and she started to blush.

"Thank you, Michael," Sarah replied. "Y-you look handsome as well."

"Thank you, my dear," replied Michael. "Coming from you, that is the highest compliment. Father Thomas, I do believe we are ready!"

Father Thomas's spirit appeared before the altar. With sadness in his dark, ghostly eyes, he turned toward Sarah.

"I'm sorry, my child," he told her. "I wish I wasn't being forced into joining you in this unholy union."

Michael became furious and stared down Father Thomas in anger.

"Just get on with it, Father," growled Michael. "We don't need your opinion."

"Who gives this woman in matrimony?" asked Father Thomas.

All eyes were on Robert, but with a stoic look upon his face, he didn't say a word.

"We can just skip this part," said Michael. "I don't think the father of the bride feels much like participating."

"Fine," said Father Thomas solemnly. "Then let us begin. Do you, Michael James Winworth, take this woman, Sarah Jane Gilmore, to be your eternally wedded wife, to have and to hold, from this day forth, to love, honor, and cherish, forsaking all others for all eternity?"

Michael looked at Sarah and smiled.

"I do," he replied.

Father Thomas then looked at the vows written for him to give to Sarah. He closed his eyes. For some reason, he didn't seem to want to read them.

"Read the vows, Father!" Michael said impatiently.

Father Thomas sighed.

"Do you, Sarah Jane Gilmore ..." Father Thomas began. "Take this man, Michael James Winworth, to be your eternally wedded husband, to have and to hold, from this day forth, to love honor and to ... to obey, to freely give him your eternal soul, as well as your free will, forsaking all others for all eternity?"

The entire room went silent.

"Damn it, Michael!" screamed Jason. "I knew you had a devious plan."

"I will not have cursing at my wedding, Brother!" Michael yelled in anger.

"Wh-what do those vows mean?" asked Sarah.

"It's simple," replied Jason. "You see, Sarah, the life-force controls the void. That would mean you, not Michael, would be in control of it. That's why he chose himself as the life-force two hundred years ago. But Pauline killed him before the void could be completed. If you agree to those vows, he not only controls the void, but he can control you too."

Sarah looked horrified. "I thought you loved me?" she asked.

"I do, Sarah, more than anything," he replied. "But I will be the one in charge. I'm afraid I can't let you have that power. Plus, I just want to make sure you will always be happy."

"By controlling me?" she asked. "Do you really think that turning me into a puppet would make me happy?" Tears began to stream down her face.

He then gently grasped her shoulders with his cold, ghostly hands and looked her straight in the eyes.

"No, Sarah," cried Michael. "I love you. I would never try to control you like that. But I could take away any pain you've experienced in the past. I can make you forget about those men who attacked you. I can make you forget anything that's too painful to remember."

"But I don't want to forget any of that," she replied. "You have no right to do that to me."

"You fucking son of a bitch!" screamed Robert. "Get your filthy hands off of my daughter!"

Michael became angry and glared at Robert. He then squeezed his hand into a fist and froze Robert. This also silenced him.

"No!" cried Sarah. "Please let my father go!"

"Sarah," cried Michael, "if you don't say, 'I do,' right now, I will have no choice but to kill him! Please don't make me do something we'll both regret. If I kill your father, your uncle is next. After that, I will make you watch as I kill everyone in this worthless town until you say it."

Frozen in fear, Sarah remained silent.

"Sarah, I'm waiting!" he cried.

Still terrified, she couldn't bring herself to say anything.

"Fine, then we'll do things the hard way!" exclaimed Michael.

He stared at Robert intensely, forcing him to stop breathing. Robert then began to levitate. Remembering that it was the same way he killed her attackers, right before Michael had covered her eyes, she cried out in horror.

"Stop!" she cried. "I do! I do! I do! Please don't hurt my father!"

With that, Michael let him go, and Robert fell to the floor. He let out a gasp of air, but he was still alive. Sarah couldn't stop crying.

"Daddy!" she screamed.

As she went to help him, Michael grabbed her gently.

"In a second, my dear," he said. "Father, finish the ceremony."

"Then by the power vested in me, I now pronounce you eternal husband and wife," said Father Thomas. "You my now kiss the bride."

With that, Michael became corporeal, as actual human flesh began to envelope his ghostly form. He grabbed Sarah and passionately kissed her. This time, however, she did not return his passion.

Then, all of a sudden, the manor started to change, just as Michael had hoped. The decaying structure and foundation gradually began to renew itself. The dead, cold, ugly darkness of the house was being replaced by warmth and a new sense of life. The structure had indeed returned to its magnificent glory. Soon after, the trapped souls became corporeal again, the same way that Michael had. Immediately a teary Jonathan ran over to Karen, as they were both crying. They threw their arms around one another and shared a loving, warm embrace.

Robert was slowly recovering from Michael's attack and steadily made his way back up onto his feet. Sarah pulled herself away from Michael's hold on her and went to her father.

"Daddy, are you okay?" she cried. She then grabbed her father, and they held each other tight.

"I'm fine, sweetheart," cried Robert. "I'm sorry I failed you."

"You didn't, Daddy," replied Sarah as she gently stroked her father's face. "You didn't."

***

Jonathan was still holding Karen, both of them crying in one another's arms. But Jonathan knew that their reunion was to be short-lived.

"All right," said Jonathan, "we had an agreement. I would give you Sarah in exchange for letting Karen and Todd go free."

Michael looked at him and smirked.

"First of all, I never said anything about releasing Todd," said Michael. "Second, because of your incompetence, Sarah was practically gang raped. You begged me for one more chance, and I gave it to you. If you didn't fail, I would not torture Karen and Todd for all eternity. You didn't fail, and so they won't be tortured."

"What!" cried Jonathan. "I've destroyed my family. I've ruined my life. I'm probably going to jail. I can't believe you're going to renege on our deal."

"I can, and I will," replied Michael in an eerily calm tone. "You kept making mistakes, and my now wife was badly hurt because of it. I'm afraid you have to pay."

"Please!" cried Jonathan. "Then at least let me stay. I'll serve you."

"Really, Jonathan, begging?" replied Michael. "Now, is that any way for a mayor to act? Besides, I'm already letting Robert stay. I don't think I could stomach both of you. Anyway, I believe Karen and Jason have grown quite fond of one another. I guess I do owe my brother at least one favor."

"You lousy, rotten son of a—" Jonathan began to say.

"Enough, Jonathan!" exclaimed Michael as he interrupted him. "We all know what my mother was. Now, this void will be closing soon. You're not coming along. I suggest you leave while you have the chance. Something bad might happen to you. The rest of you may retire to your quarters.

Robert, I'm sure you'll find plenty of room in the east wing. My beautiful wife and I are going to consummate our union. Good night."

Before Michael had a chance to grab Sarah from her father's embrace, Jonathan grabbed her first. It happened so fast neither Robert nor Sarah realized what was happening.

He wrapped his arm around her neck and pulled out a dagger. Michael recognized it right away. It was the same danger that was used to sacrifice Jason two hundred years earlier. Jonathan then pressed the dagger right over Sarah's heart.

"Release Karen and Todd at once, Michael!" cried Jonathan. "Or I swear I'll stab her right in the heart!"

***

CHAPTER 26
Sins of the Past

Michael became angry. He felt hatred toward Jonathan. Now more than ever, he wanted to kill him.

"Where did you get that?" cried Michael.

"Why don't you ask Father Thomas?" Jonathan responded.

"My son, you don't want to do this," said Father Thomas.

"I have no choice, Father," said Jonathan. "I don't want to hurt Sarah, but I have been brought to my breaking point. Did you really think that I would be dumb enough to trust you, Michael?"

"Jonathan, what the hell are you doing?" cried Robert.

"I'm sorry, Robert," said Jonathan, "but we're talking one lost soul for hundreds imprisoned here."

"What do you mean lost soul?" asked Robert.

"Sarah's soul and the void are one," Michael explained. "That dagger is the only thing that can kill her, but it can't harm anyone else in here. Since it created the void, it can destroy it. If he drives it into her heart, the void will cease to exist. Sarah will also cease to exist because her soul would be destroyed. Sarah would face complete oblivion."

"Jonathan, don't do this!" cried Robert.

"I'm sorry, Robert," cried Jonathan, "but I have nothing else to lose. You said it yourself; I'm dead to you."

"Jonathan," cried Karen, "please don't do this!"

"I'm sorry, Karen," said Jonathan. "I'd rather have you hate me than have you trapped here forever. Also with the void destroyed, everyone goes free. Then Michael ends up in hell where he belongs."

"Don't do this, my son," said Father Thomas.

"You had the answer the whole time, Father," said Jonathan, "but you didn't use it."

"I save souls," Father Thomas responded. "I don't destroy them. This girl has suffered enough. Please do not hurt her."

"I don't want to," cried Jonathan, "but so many people have suffered because of Michael. I read your notes. I know everything. Why don't you tell everyone here how you came into possession of the dagger?"

Father Thomas sighed, and he began to reveal what had happened. "It was the night that Michael first tried to create the void," Father Thomas began.

***

Two Hundred Years Prior

Father Thomas was at the seminary getting reading for bed. It was at that moment he heard a frantic knock on the door.

"Father Thomas!" a young woman cried. "Father Thomas! Please, help me!" He opened the door and immediately recognized the frightened young woman. She was disheveled and covered in blood.

"Pauline, what happened?" he asked her.

"Look!" she cried.

She then pointed to the manor. There was a strange, ungodly explosion, one like he had never seen. A burst of fire and lightning shot up into the night sky. The sky was lit ablaze. It looked as though hell itself had engulfed the manor.

"Father, you have to help me!" cried Pauline. "You have to help Jason. He's trapped in there!"

"Come in, my child," he told her. "Now tell me what happened."

"Michael invited us over for dinner, but it was a trap," she began.

Pauline continued to tell him all that had transpired. "Jason's soul is trapped in there forever. You have to get his soul out of there, Father!"

"Is that the dagger?" he asked.

She looked down at the dagger in her hand.

"Oh my God!" she exclaimed. "I didn't even realize I still had it! I'm a murderer!"

"Pauline, it sounds more like self-defense," he replied, "but I can absolve you of that sin, and I'm sure God will understand."

"Father, please save Jason!" she cried.

"I will try," he began. "I have been trained to exorcise demons, but I'm not sure it will work on the evil spirit of a witch. In the meantime, I think it would be best if you stayed at the convent. You can get a bath and hide among the sisters. We may need to burn that dress. I don't want the authorities finding out about this. They may not be as understanding."

"Father," asked Pauline, "can you do me one more favor? Can you give me Last Rites?"

"What?" he asked. His eyes widened as he quickly looked her way. Before he even had a chance to answer her, she had plunged the dagger into her abdomen.

"*No!*" he cried. He ran over to her and grabbed her as she hit the ground. He then cradled her dying body.

"Why, Pauline? Why?" he cried.

"Father," she said, "pl-please send my Jason back to me."

She let out one last breath, her body went limp, and with that, she was gone. He held her lifeless body close to his and continued to cry. He then gave her Last Rites and absolved her of her sins. She was secretly buried in an unmarked grave.

He felt that he had failed both Pauline and Jason. No matter what it took, he had to make it right. So he began to study Michael's family history. The dagger had been in Michael's maternal family for generations.

Father Thomas tried to destroy the dagger, but nothing worked. He couldn't even melt it. There was powerful dark magic protecting it, so it could not be destroyed. So he buried it in the seminary with the hopes that it would never be found.

***

Present Day

"It took me a year to try to figure out a way to exorcise the manor," explained Father Thomas. "It was a combination of previous exorcist training and reading up on Michael's maternal side of his family that helped me put together a plan. I was even in correspondence with Pope

Pius VII himself. But it didn't matter what I did. I failed, and I have been trapped here for almost two centuries. How did you find it?"

"The seminary closed over a century ago," said Jonathan. "The dagger and all your notes were discovered when the entire area was excavated a few years ago. The town didn't know what to do with it. They knew what it was, and they feared it. So those in charge, at the time, locked it away in a vault at city hall."

"My God!" cried Robert. "Is that what you picked up from your office?"

"I was hoping that it wouldn't come to this, Robert, but I needed a backup plan," said Jonathan.

"Jonathan!" cried Karen. "Sarah's like a daughter to me. If you don't release Sarah right now, I'm done with you!"

"I'm sorry, Karen!" cried Jonathan. "I love Sarah! I don't want to hurt her! But I love you more! I would do anything to save you! Even if it means killing my own Goddaughter or killing your love for me!"

"If you think you're getting out of here alive, Jonathan," snarled Michael, "think again!"

"You can't scare me, Michael!" exclaimed Jonathan. "Because right now, I have your only weakness, Sarah! Now do you let Karen and Todd go, or do I have to destroy my own niece?"

Sarah closed her eyes as warm tears began to stream down her face. The family that she had always loved and trusted was now falling apart before her very eyes.

"You bastard!" cried Robert. He then punched Jonathan in the face. Jonathan quickly went down, releasing Sarah and dropping the dagger. A furious Michael grabbed Jonathan by the neck and lifted him off of the ground.

"Now you will die!" screamed Michael.

"Stop!" yelled Sarah, holding the dagger to her heart. "If you don't let him go right now, I'm going to drive this damn thing into my own heart!"

***

CHAPTER 27
Conflict and Compromise

"I said let him go, Michael!" cried Sarah. "I'm not going to let you kill another person. There've been too many deaths. No more, this ends now!"

For the first time in her life, she found her own inner strength. Sarah was determined to stop Michael from hurting any more people. Now she was the one in control.

"Okay, Sarah, I won't kill him," said Michael. "Just give me the dagger."

Michael gazed at her as tears began welling up in his eyes. Sarah just shook her head.

"No!" she cried. "I don't believe you. Don't even think about trying to command me into giving it to you! This dagger is just over my heart! If I sense any sort of mind manipulation from you, it's going right in! Now, Michael, do you really want to test to see which one of us will be quicker?"

"Sarah, don't do this!" cried Robert. He then turned his attention toward Michael. "Look what you've done to her! Look what you've done to everyone! My daughter's about to kill herself because of you!"

"Sarah, please don't do this!" cried Michael with tears streaming down his face.

"Why? Because it will destroy your precious void?" she asked. "The one you had to create, no matter how many people you hurt? How many more people do you have to go through to get what you want? I refuse to be a part of that! I'd rather no longer exist than spend eternity with a monster!"

"To hell with the void!" screamed Michael. "Sarah, it's not even worth having without you! I love you, Sarah! I can't stand the thought of you being wiped from existence! What do you want? Do you want me to expel myself from the manor? If I leave, I will revert back to a soul. I'll probably end up in hell. But if I'm not with you, I'll be in hell anyway. Is that what you want? Say the word, and I will leave. I will be out of your life forever. But please, don't destroy the beautiful young woman who stands here before me. Do you really hate me, Sarah?" He stared at her with more tears in his eyes.

She said nothing but continued to cry. A feeling of both sadness and rage was building up inside of her. Sarah just kept looking at him.

"Yes!" she screamed, "*I do hate you*! I hate the way you causally kill innocent people! I even hate what you're doing to those men in the cellar, despite what they did to me! I hate that you tore my family apart! I hate the way you treat those you have enslaved here! I hate what you did to my aunt and her brother. I hate what you did to your own brother and his wife! I hate that you took advantage of my own sexual desires!"

A look of devastation spread across Michael's face. His eyes widened, and his face was just frozen in utter disbelief.

"Sarah!" Michael cried, "Please—" but before he could continue, she interrupted him.

Tears continued streaming down her cheeks.

"But do you want to know the one thing, Michael," Sarah replied, "the one thing that I hate the most? I hate the fact that I also love you! Despite all the horrible things you've done, God help me, I really do love you! I've loved you since I first looked at this place. I felt a connection with you! That's why it was so easy to seduce me! And that's why I let you comfort me when I needed it. You have a gentle side, but for some reason, you only show it to me!"

Again, his tear-filled eyes widened, but this time, he had a glimmer of hope.

"Sarah!" cried Michael. "If you love me, we can be happy!"

"It's not that simple!" she replied. "I love you, but I hate you at the same time. I love the gentlemen, but I hate the monster. I'm not spending eternity with a bunch of hapless slaves being bullied by you! And I could never treat them as servants. If you continue to be a gentlemen, my love for you will only grow. If you continue to be a sadistic monster, it'll be my hatred that grows. I'm not spending eternity like that. But I wouldn't mind spending eternity with the man who lovingly held me after I was attacked.

That's why I don't want you to take away that memory. It reminds me of why I love you and why I want to be with you."

***

"Sarah!" replied Michael, "I love you. Despite the darkness that I know is inside of me, I do love you." He closed his eyes as tears began to stream down his face. Michael was now breathing heavily, trying to hold back the tears.

With the dagger still in her left hand and still pointing toward her own heart, she gently placed her right hand on his cheek. He opened his eyes and saw that she also had tears in her eyes. But she soon gave him a loving smile. No one else had ever looked at him like that. Michael couldn't stop crying.

"All it was, that you ever really wanted, was just to feel loved," Sarah cried. "Wasn't it?" She smiled and began to lovingly caress his face.

As Michael continued crying, he gently placed his hand on top of hers. He held her hand against his cheek and slowly closed his eyes. Michael nodded and then opened them. He looked right into Sarah's eyes and then kissed the palm of her hand. "You're my everything, Sarah!" cried Michael.

"Please, Michael, give me a reason to want to love you," she cried.

"Whatever you want, Sarah," proclaimed Michael. "I promise my only wish is to grant your every heart's desire."

"Then let them go, Michael!" she demanded. "Let them all go! Jason, my aunt, even the men in the cellar. Just please let them all go and spare my uncle as well. After you set them free, then I will give you the dagger. Then, and only then, can we begin this marriage. I promise I'll be a loving wife, but prove to me why I should be. Please, just set them all free."

"If that's what you want, Sarah," replied Michael, "then that's what I'll do. You're all that matters."

He began to compose himself and turned his attention to all those he had imprisoned over the years.

"You are all free to go! I release all of you!" exclaimed Michael. With that, all his victims headed for the front door.

As they made their way through the exit, a burst of white light engulfed them, and their corporeal bodies disappeared. In the blink of an eye, they were gone. Finally free from the manor and Michael's tyranny, the souls were released.

"Sarah," said Michael, "please give me the dagger."

Sarah lowered it from her chest and then handed it to Michael.

Karen, Todd, Jason, and Father Thomas had yet to leave the manor and were still in their corporeal bodies.

"Why are you still here?" asked Michael. "Why haven't you left?"

"We want to say goodbye," replied Jason.

"Well then, goodbye," said Michael sarcastically.

"Not to you," said a disgusted Father Thomas.

He then turned his attention toward Sarah and gently took her hand. "I believe that God calls all his children home to him. You will not be an exception. Yes, you pledged your eternal soul to Michael but not to Satan. Also, you did it to save those you love and even those who hurt you. God will understand that, and he will eventually find you. Despite what Michael's ego believes, God is much more powerful than he is. For if anyone belongs in God's heavenly kingdom, it's you, my child." He then turned his attention to Michael.

"As for you, Michael," Father Thomas began, "may God have mercy on your soul because I know I sure as hell wouldn't!" He then headed toward the door. As he left the manor, his soul was set free.

Jason then walked up to Sarah, looked at her, and smiled.

"It has been an honor and a privilege to make your acquaintance," he told her. "For you truly are a lady. Only a special angel could make a demon cry."

He then kissed the back of her hand.

Sarah gave him a sweet smile. "Go be with Pauline," she told him.

He smiled back at her and gave her a wink. His demeanor turned cold and then changed to angry when he looked at his brother.

"As far as I'm concerned, we stopped being brothers the night you separated me from my wife," Jason spat. "That being said, I am going to offer you one last piece of brotherly advice—not for you but for Sarah. Not that you deserve her love or deserve to be happy. However, I hope you two do find happiness together. If anyone deserves it, it's her. Otherwise, I would wish you nothing but pain and grief. Treat her like a person and not a possession. Then maybe, just maybe, this entire nightmare can work out. But just one more thing, brother!"

With that, his fist came flying across the left side of Michael's face. As soon as it made contact, Michael fell to the ground. He lay there with a stunned look upon his face.

"That was for the last two hundred years!" he spat. "And also for Pauline!" Michael looked up at Jason, rubbing his injury, and just glared at him. As much as Michael wanted to hurt Jason, he did nothing. He didn't want to upset Sarah. So, he slowly got back up off of the floor but did not seek retribution.

As Jason left the manor, he smiled and winked at Karen before walking out the door. She smiled back. His friendship with her made their less-than-ideal situation a little bit more tolerable.

Karen and Todd then made their way to Sarah.

"Thank you, Sarah!" said Karen. "You were the closest I ever had to a daughter. I will always love you. And I'm sorry that Jonathan hurt you. Even though it was for me, I wish he hadn't betrayed you. Even though Michael doesn't deserve it, I hope you two will be very happy."

"Aunt Karen, can you do me a favor?" asked Sarah.

"Anything, sweetheart," Karen replied with a smile.

"C-can you tell my mother that I love her?" asked a teary-eyed Sarah.

"Of course," said Karen, "but I have a feeling she already knows."

"Well, then just tell her I said, 'Hi!'" Sarah replied with a smile.

With that, they shared a loving embrace, and Karen gave her a peck on the cheek. She then made her way to Robert.

"Take care of yourself, Robert," said Karen. She was smiling but with tears in her eyes.

"I will," said Robert, smiling back at her. "You were always an exceptional person and never deserved any of this. I'm glad that your soul will find peace."

"Goodbye, Robert," Todd said as he shook Robert's hand. "You've raised a beautiful girl. Helen would be proud of you." Todd then made his way to Sarah, while Michael just glared at him.

"Sarah," said Todd, "I would have waited for you to turn twenty-one. But as I paraphrased John Lennon, 'Life is what happens when you start making plans.' John Lennon was probably my favorite Monkee."

They looked at each other and laughed. Sarah placed her hands on his shoulders and a peck on his cheek. He smiled at her before giving her one final embrace.

Todd then turned his attention toward Michael.

"Take care of her," Todd told him. "She is very special and should be treated as such."

"I assure you, my angel will have the best of everything," he said, annoyed.

"Goodbye, Todd," said Sarah. "Thanks for being my first crush." She looked at him and smiled.

Karen and Todd took one another's hand and started to leave the manor. Jonathan went up to them.

"Karen, I—" Jonathan began.

"Save it, Jonathan!" Karen said, interrupting him with anger. "You threatened a member of my family. Even though she's your blood relative, I still love her dearly. I know you did it for me, but almost sacrificing Sarah's life wasn't worth it. I'm sorry for what has happened to you. I'm sorry it turned you into someone I could no longer love."

"Karen," cried Jonathan. He looked at her and began to cry. But she just stared at him with a cold look upon her face.

"Goodbye, Jonathan," Karen stated without emotion.

She and Todd were still holding hands. They left the manor together. They too had their souls released and made their way to their final destinations.

Sarah began to cry, and Michael wrapped his arms around her in a loving embrace.

"Robert? Sarah?" Jonathan inquired.

They just ignored him. They were both done with him.

"Nobody wants you here, Jonathan!" exclaimed Michael.

"Maybe, but at least Karen and Todd are free," replied Jonathan. "All it cost me was her love, the love of the rest of my family, and my reputation. But it was a sacrifice I had to make."

"Leave, Jonathan!" yelled Michael. "The void is about to close. And take this thing with you! I don't want it anywhere near Sarah ever again!"

He then threw the dagger near Jonathan's feet. Jonathan picked up the dagger and left through the front door. Robert went to his daughter.

As he approached her, Sarah released herself from Michael's arms. They then shared a tight and loving embrace. This did not make Michael happy.

"Sarah!" cried Robert. "I was afraid I was going to lose you forever." He embraced his daughter and kissed her cheek. She also took in his loving embrace.

"Oh, Daddy!" cried Sarah. "I love you so much!"

Michael just glared at them.

"Sarah," said Michael, "it's time to say good night to your father. As I said, the east wing will be more than sufficient for you, Robert. I will let you know when you can see my wife, but it's our wedding night. Sarah did promise to be a good wife, and she shall be. Come, my love. It's time for you to give yourself to me."

"Like hell she will!" cried Robert.

"I beg your pardon?" Michael responded in anger.

"Daddy, please!" cried Sarah. "What are you doing? We have an agreement!"

"Sarah, you are sixteen years old!" cried Robert. "I am your legal guardian. This marriage is null and void. And any agreements you made, he can't force you to keep! We're leaving!" He then grabbed Sarah by the upper arm and headed for the front door.

"Daddy, stop! You don't understand!" Sarah pleaded with her father.

"Stop!" yelled Michael. "This is your last warning! If you try to take her out that door, you'll never see her again! As I've stated before, your laws don't apply here! Sarah cannot leave the manor!"

"Fuck you!" cried Robert. "I am her father! There is no way in hell I'm letting a pervert like you have your way with my daughter!"

"Daddy, stop!" cried Sarah. "Please don't anger him!" She kept trying to pull away from her father, but he wouldn't release her. As they got to the front door, Robert attempted to push her out the door. But a force field was blocking him. Michael had just made his way over to them.

"Let down this damn force field!" yelled Robert.

"Oh, I'm afraid I can't do that," replied a smug Michael. "You know, people really need to learn proper English. If you don't use some words correctly, it can lead to misunderstandings—like the words *can* and *may*. Most people seem to mix up those two words quite a lot. You see, when I said she *cannot* leave the manor, I meant that literally. As the word *cannot* is actually supposed to be used. The manor is the void, and Sarah and the void are one. So I also mean it when I say I can't let down the force field, because it's not a force field. That came down as soon as Sarah's life-force created the void. The only thing the manor is keeping in here is Sarah."

"Please give him another chance!" cried Sarah.

"I'm sorry, my dear," replied Michael. "But he has tested my patience for the last time. I warned him, but he didn't listen."

"Please don't take my daughter from me!" begged Robert. "I'll do anything." He looked at Michael, pleading while he felt tears well up in his eyes.

Michael flashed him a wicked smile.

"You know, normally when someone says that to me, I usually degrade them," explained Michael. "Then, I make them pathetically beg, and I give them false hope. And after they've made fools out of themselves, I reveal that I never promised them anything. But don't worry, Robert, I promise I won't do that to you."

"Thank you," replied Robert, as he started to compose himself.

"My pleasure," replied Michael with a smile, "For, you see, I'm just not in the mood for any silly mind games. And you're just not worth my time. So I'm afraid it's time for you to go!" Michael face hardened, and with just wave of his hand, Robert flew out the front door. With a loud thud, Robert crash-landed on the now rain-soaked ground.

Sarah tried to run to her father.

"Daddy!" cried Sarah. More than anything, Sarah wanted her father. But the manor itself wouldn't let her leave. She and the void were now one entity. She kept crying and banging on the invisible barrier that was separating her from her father. Angry and crying, Sarah turned to Michael.

"Why!" she screamed, with tears pouring down her cheeks. "Please let him back in!"

"I'm sorry, my dear," Michael replied. "Just as you can't leave the void, he cannot come back in here. Once the void is created, nothing outside of it can enter. Your father disrespected me for the last time. We should not be disrespected in our own home."

"Sarah!" cried Robert as he made his way back to the door. Both Robert and Sarah placed their hands on the invisible barrier. They were both crying. This was the closest they'd ever get to one another. Michael then stood behind Sarah. Robert became infuriated.

"You rotten son of a bitch!" Robert cried. "How dare you take my daughter away from me!"

Michael ignored him and gently grabbed Sarah's upper arm.

"Come, my dear," said Michael. "It's time for us to go."

"No! Don't touch me!" she cried, as she jerked away from his grasp. "You didn't have to do this! It didn't have to be this way! You didn't really want him to stay, did you? You were jealous of our relationship! I thought you could change, but you can't. You won't! You never will! *I hate you!*"

Michael just continued to look at her with a loving smile.

"My dear, hate is just another form of passion," he replied in a loving voice. "You wouldn't hate me so much right now if you didn't love me."

"*No!*" she screamed. "I said I loved the gentleman, but that's not really you! That will never be you! I will never love a narcissistic demon like you! *I hate you!*"

Slap! Her open hand came right across his face.

Michael, with a completely shocked look in his eyes, placed his hand on his burning red cheek. Sarah widened her eyes in fear. She looked like a deer caught in headlights, stunned by what had just occurred. She was obviously afraid of what he might try to do to her.

Michael then grabbed Sarah, but he was gentle and did not harm her. He kept his word. For he truly did love her unconditionally and would never harm her. Jason had been right; Sarah was the only one who could have gotten away with that.

Instead of becoming violent, Michael wrapped his arms around her. He then pulled her into a firm yet loving embrace. He held her tight as she tried to wriggle her way out of his grasp.

"Let me go, you monster!" she cried. "Please, let me go!"

Robert began pounding on the invisible barrier at the front door.

"Sarah!" Robert cried. "Let go of her, you pedophile!"

But instead, Michael just held her closer to him. He gently placed his hand on the back of her head and eased it into the crook of his neck.

"Shh …" Michael began. "Shh … I'm here, Sarah. I'm here. Don't be frightened. I promise, my love, everything is going to be all right. It's okay, Sarah. It's okay. Everything is going to be fine."

He was now rubbing her back, as he was trying to comfort her. Sarah just kept crying and kept struggling as she tried desperately to escape his strong grasp. But he refused to release her from his embrace.

Exhausted from fighting him, both her mind and her body lost the will to fight. Sarah slowly began to drop to the floor as she continued to cry.

Michael had a look of concern and compassion upon his face. While still holding her in his arms, he slowly made his way down to the floor with her. He kept holding her tight as he gently began to rock her.

"Shh," whispered Michael. "It's okay, Sarah. You're okay. I love you so much." He then placed a kiss upon her left temple.

"Sarah! What are you doing?" cried Robert. By then, he was a mess. Tears just kept flowing from his eyes.

Michael then slowly pulled away from Sarah, but they were still holding one another. He cupped her chin with his hand and had a puzzled look upon his face.

"Sarah, why are you crying?" he asked in a soft tone. "It's our wedding night. I was hoping you'd be happy."

"I'm … I'm sorry," she replied. "I guess I just miss my mom. I'm just glad I was able to make peace with her."

Robert couldn't believe what was unfolding before his eyes. "Sarah!" he cried. "Sarah, that's not why!" For some reason, Sarah couldn't hear him.

"Is there anything else bothering you, Sarah?" asked Michael, with a lot of interest in his eyes.

A cold, yet angry expression appeared on her face. "My father!" she spat.

"What about your father?" asked Michael.

Tears began to stream down her cheeks. "I don't understand," she said as she looked into Michael's eyes. "Why? How-how could he? How could he leave my mother for a younger woman when my mother was six months pregnant with me?"

Robert's eyes became as wide as saucers.

"*What*?" cried Robert. "Sarah, that's not true! You have to know that's not true! I love you and your mother more than anything! I would never leave you!"

"But you know what really hurts?" said Sarah. "The fact that he never had anything to do with me."

"Oh God, Sarah!" cried Robert. "I'm right here! Why are you believing these lies? Why?"

Oh my God! Her wedding vows!

"Sarah," cried Robert, as he continued banging on the barrier, "he's in your head! You gave him your free will! He's manipulating you through your mind! Sarah!"

But she could not hear him, and Michael continued to ignore him. He just acted as though Robert wasn't even there. Michael stood up off of the floor and looked down at Sarah.

"You know what, Sarah?" said Michael. "Sometimes a person just doesn't know what he has until it's too late. There are consequences for one's actions. Unfortunately, most people don't learn this lesson in time."

As he continued to talk, he extended his hands to her and gave her a loving smile.

Sarah smiled back at him and gladly took his hands as they had been offered to her. With that, he eagerly, yet gently, pulled her back up onto her feet and into his loving embrace.

"But the good news is, Sarah, your father's loss is my gain," Michael continued. "I get you all to myself, and you and I are going to be very happy."

As they held one another, they stared into each other's eyes. Sarah was so elated by his words, as well as his actions, that she couldn't help but smile.

"Now then, my dear, do you remember when I entered your dreams?" Michael asked her.

She looked at Michael and gave him a devilish smile. He began to place open-mouthed kisses upon her neck. She closed her eyes and tilted her head back.

"Yes," she replied with arousal in her voice.

"Do you remember how good I made you feel?" Michael asked in a husky whisper. He began to untie the laces on the back of her wedding gown.

"Yes," she replied with a pleased sigh.

Michael kept continuously kissing her neck. She closed her eyes and began to moan.

"Stop!" screamed Robert. "Get away from my daughter, you pervert! Sarah! Wake up, Sarah!"

But she just couldn't hear his pleas. Her gown slipped off of her body and down to the floor. From the waist up, she was completely naked. The only thing she had on was a pair of white silk underwear.

Right in front of her own father, Michael began caressing her right breast while kissing her passionately on the lips. Then, like a ravenous carnivore's, his lips began devouring her neck. This made Sarah moan even more.

"Do you want me to take you upstairs?" Michael asked in a sensual whisper. "Do you want me to make you feel that good again?"

"Yes," she replied. She opened her eyes and gave him a seductive smile.

Michael looked down at her and then noticed the locket. With that, he grabbed and ripped it off of her neck. This caused her to let out a pleased sigh. He let the locket hang off of his index finger, as he seemed to be intensely studying it.

"You know, my dear," Michael began. "A woman as lovely as you does deserve the finest of jewelry—much finer than this! Besides, it's not like it has any sentimental value." He then looked at Robert and gave him a wickedly triumphant smile. With that, he tossed it out the door, and it landed at Robert's feet.

"No! Don't you dare erase me from Sarah's memory!" cried Robert, and he fell to his knees. "Sarah!" But she could not hear him.

Michael then scooped her up into his arms, and they stared lovingly into one another's eyes.

"Michael?" Sarah asked.

"What is it, my love?" he replied. "As I stated earlier, my only wish is to grant your every heart's desire."

"Remember when you orally pleasured me on the beach?" she asked.

"Oh my God!" cried Robert, aggressively running his fingers through his hair.

"Of course, my dear," he responded with a smile on his face.

"Perhaps this time," she said with a devilishly seductive smile, "maybe I could return the favor!"

His face then returned her smile.

"As I said before, my love," he responded, "my only wish is to grant your every heart's desire. I love you, Sarah."

"I love you too, Michael," she replied.

They looked at one another with loving smiles. With her arms wrapped around the back of Michael's neck, she lay her head against his shoulder. She then closed her eyes and let him lovingly cradle her in his arms. Michael then turned his attention toward Robert.

"She's right, you know," said Michael. "It didn't have to be this way. But as I said to her, 'Sometimes a person doesn't know what they have until it's too late.' You shouldn't have crossed me as you did. I warned you, Robert. My own brother tried to warn you, as well. But you just wouldn't listen."

"What difference would it have made?" cried Robert.

"Plenty," replied Michael. "You see, I was willing to work with you. I was willing to let you stay, for her. But to be honest, I am glad things turned out this way. She was right. I was jealous of her love for you. And I don't really want to share her time or her love with someone else, even her own father. That's why there will be no children. For you see, I truly am an extremely selfish man, a true son of a bitch, but you already knew that."

Still in tears, Robert looked at both of them in disbelief.

"Sarah!" cried Robert. But her eyes remained closed, as she was still in complete and utter ignorant bliss. She was completely oblivious to her father's presence.

"I'm afraid she can't hear you," said Michael. "I know that you think I'm just doing this to be sadistic. I will admit, I am enjoying this. But this for the best. It'll be easier on her, in the long run."

"No!" cried Robert, "You mean it will be easier on you! Maybe you manipulated her into not hating you! But you know damn good and well that this is going to hurt her. Her mother is gone, and she now thinks I never wanted to be her father! My own daughter, whom I love more than anything! She thinks I never wanted to love her! Do you really think that isn't going to cause her some great amount of pain?"

Michael flashed Robert a wicked smile.

"Well then, my dear father-in-law," replied Michael, "I guess it's good that she has such an adoring husband, one who will always offer her a loving shoulder to cry on. Well, at least on the rare occasions when she will actually need it."

Michael continued to look at his broken father-in-law. An evil smirk appeared upon his face as he stared at the man he had completely destroyed.

"Now then, I am going to take my beautiful wife upstairs to the bridal suite," said Michael. "There, we will consummate our happy union, by making passionate love to one another. Hopefully, we won't wear ourselves out too much. As for you, my dear father-in-law, if I were you, I would get one last good look at her. Because you will never *ever* be seeing her again."

"Bastard!" screamed Robert. Once again, he began to bang his fists on the invisible barrier, as if it was a last-ditch effort to get his daughter's attention.

"Sarah!" cried Robert. For a brief moment, there was a glimmer of hope. Sarah lifted her head from Michael's shoulder and opened her eyes.

"Did you hear something?" she asked with a look of confusion. She kept looking around as if she was trying to figure out what she had heard and from where the sound was coming. Michael looked at her and smiled.

"Nothing to concern that pretty little head of yours," whispered Michael. "It was just an echo. It's not anything important enough for you to even acknowledge."

"Oh," Sarah whispered her reply. She then closed her eyes and smiled, as she once again rested her head on his shoulder.

Michael turned his back on Robert and began to walk away with his new bride. With that, the door on the manor closed, and just like that, the manor completely disappeared.

"*Nooooo!*" cried Robert. "*Sarahhhhh!*"

***

Chapter 28
Bittersweet Madness

"I'm sorry, Sarah!" cried Robert. "I'm sorry, Helen!" He was sitting on his knees, rain pouring down on him. Yet the rain was no match for his own tears. As he looked down, he saw the locket. He picked it up and opened it.

"No!" he cried, looking at the picture of his late wife. "I failed you, Helen! I didn't protect our baby girl!" Robert then looked up at where the manor once was. There was such bitter irony. More than anything, he had wanted to have it demolished. Now it was gone. All that was left was a giant hole—but not as big as the one in his heart.

He kept screaming and crying, in emotional agony. His beloved daughter, Sarah, had forever been taken from him. But what was worse was the fact that she would never remember him. She would never remember how much he loved her. As far as she was concerned, he had been nothing more than a cheating, deadbeat dad. How was he supposed to go on now?

"Robert!" he heard a familiar voice cry.

Robert turned around and saw Jonathan running toward him. Robert began to seethe with rage. His adrenaline started to increase, and he could feel his entire body heat up.

"You fucking rat bastard!" Robert cried. "I swear I'm gonna kill you!"

Jonathan held up his hands, trying to shield himself from Robert. But then, with a hard right hook, Robert punched the left side of Jonathan's face. Jonathan went down before he even knew what hit him. In a blind rage, Robert got on top of Jonathan and began to strangle him.

"Robert, stop," said Jonathan, gasping for air. He looked up and couldn't believe the hatred in his brother's eyes.

"This is all your fault, Jonathan!" cried Robert. "Not only is Sarah gone, but she doesn't even know who I am! That son of a bitch erased me from her memory!" He then let go of Jonathan's neck as Jonathan started gasping for air. At that moment, Robert noticed the dagger lying next to his brother. Jonathan must have dropped it when Robert hit him. Robert straddled his still weakened brother. Still coughing, Jonathan was horrified by the look in Robert's eyes. Robert stared at him with hatred and malevolence.

"You're going to get me back into that house!" cried Robert, holding the dagger straight down toward his brother. Jonathan tried to move, but Robert's weight was too much.

"No!" pleaded Jonathan. "Robert, we're brothers. I love you! Besides, it won't work that—" Before he could even finish the sentence, Robert had plunged the dagger into his heart. To Robert's dismay, the manor did not return. Out of anger, hatred, and ultimate rage, he kept plunging the dagger over and over again into Jonathan's lifeless body. Blood was shooting up all around him.

"Why … won't … this … work?" screamed Robert. He just kept stabbing him until he ran out of energy. As he began profusely sweating and breathing heavily, his emotions de-escalated. He then looked in horror at what he had just done. Jonathan was unrecognizable. Robert had not only stabbed him in the chest but his face as well. He crawled off of his brother's lifeless corpse and vomited. He didn't even remember stabbing Jonathan.

"Jonathan!" he cried. "Oh God, what have I done?"

All of a sudden, a bright light shined upon him.

"Robert Gilmore!" the booming voice exclaimed.

For a split second, he thought it was God coming to judge him. After a while, he realized it was Lieutenant Johnson yelling at him through a bullhorn.

***

"Please put your hands up!" ordered Eric. "This is the police! You are under arrest!"

Robert stood up with his hands raised. He was covered in his own sweat and his brother's blood. With guns drawn, about ten police officers headed for him. Robert just stood there with a wide-eyed, blank expression upon his face. As they approached him, he had no intention to move.

"Oh my God!" exclaimed Eric when he saw what was left of Jonathan. He then looked at Robert.

"Where's Sarah?" asked Eric. "Where is she?"

Robert still didn't say a word, and he had a glazed look upon his face. With gun still drawn on him, Officer Jenkins went behind him and began to cuff his wrists.

"Robert Gilmore," Eric began, "you have the right to remain silent! Anything you say can and will be used against you in a court of law! You have the right—" But before he could get out the rest of the statement, Robert quickly grabbed Officer Jerkins and her gun. With his left arm wrapped around her neck, he held the gun to her right temple.

"Back off, Eric!" screamed Robert. "Or I swear I'll blow her fucking head off!"

"Okay, Robert," said Eric in a relaxed voice. "Let's remain calm. You don't want to do something you'll later regret."

"Tell the rest of them to back off!" ordered Robert.

Eric turned around. He then ordered the rest of the officers to lower their weapons and slowly back away.

"Okay, Robert," said Eric. "It's just you, me, and Carolyn. That's Officer Jenkins's first name, Robert. It's Carolyn. Just remember she has a father too, and it would kill him if anything ever happened to her. Tell me, Robert, what is it you want?"

"I want Sarah!" Robert cried, his face covered in tears.

"Robert, what happened to Sarah?" asked Eric.

"He took her!" cried Robert.

"Who took her, Robert?" asked Eric. "Who?"

"Michael Winworth!" Robert cried. "He forced her to marry him, made her forget who I was, and then made me watch as he molested her right in front of my eyes! And then he kept my little girl in that damn house as it went into another dimension. I'm never going to see her again! He took her away from me forever!"

"That sounds horrible, Robert," replied Eric. "I don't know what I would do if that ever happened to one of my daughters. I know Carolyn's father would be devastated if anything like that ever happened to her.

Robert, you're a father. You don't want to hurt Carolyn, do you? Would Sarah?"

Robert shook his head as he continued to cry.

"No, I don't want to hurt her," replied Robert, crying. "And Sarah wouldn't want me to hurt her either."

Eric stuck out his arms and showed the palms of his hands. He then slowly made his way toward Robert.

"Robert, listen to me," said Eric soothingly. "Put the gun down, and let Carolyn go. Too many good people have died today. We don't need any more deaths."

Robert again shook his head.

"No!" cried Robert. "There's one more!" He then kissed Carolyn on the top of her head.

"I'm so sorry, my baby girl!" cried Robert. "I'm so sorry, Sarah! But this is for the best! It's the only way to keep you safe!" He then stuck the barrel of the gun in his mouth and pulled the trigger. *Bang*!

"*No!*" screamed Eric as blood and tissue matter flew out the back of Robert's head. The weight of Robert's body forced Carolyn to fall with him. Her face was covered in Robert's splattered blood.

"Carolyn, are you all right?" asked Eric as he bent down and helped her to get back upon her feet.

Her face looked numb, and she was noticeably shaken. Carolyn was sure that Robert was going to kill her. At some point, in his obviously delusional state, he must have thought she was Sarah. But despite her harrowing ordeal, she was able to pull herself together.

"I'm fine," she replied.

It took all her mental strength, but she was able to hold back the tears that were trying to escape her eyes. However, she knew she would likely break down as soon as it all would be said and done. She was a cop—and a damn good one—but she was also human.

"Carolyn, are you sure you're all right?" asked Eric. "No one would think less of you if you weren't."

"I said, 'I'm fine,' sir," she replied while still composing herself. She then looked down at Robert. "Is he—"

"Yes," Eric replied.

"What happened to him?" she asked.

"I have no idea," he said.

Carolyn looked around. The sun was starting to rise. That was when she noticed something was wrong.

"Sir?" she asked. "Where's the manor?"

"What are you talking about, Jenkins?" he asked her. "That eyesore's where it always is. It's right … What the hell? Where the hell did it go?" He walked toward where it should have been and saw the big hole in the ground—not only was the visible part of the manor gone, but the entire foundation was as well.

"Sir?" asked Carolyn. "How did this happen?"

"I have no idea, Jenkins," he said with confusion. "I have no idea. I only know one thing. I need to get out of this nutty town."

***

The End